PURSUING THE POLITICIANS

A SPECULATIVE FICTION NOVELLA

THE NEXT HIGH PRIEST SERIES
BOOK 8

PETER DEHAAN

Pursuing the Politicians: A Speculative Fiction Novella

Copyright © 2025 by Peter DeHaan

The Next High Priest Series, Book 8.

Library of Congress Control Number: 2025914577

Published by Rock Rooster Books, Grand Rapids, Michigan

ISBNs:

- 979-8-88809-161-6 (ebook)
- 979-8-88809-162-3 (paperback)
- 979-8-88809-163-0 (audiobook)

Credits:

- Developmental editor: Julie Harbison
- Copyeditor: Robyn Mulder
- Cover design: Fanderclai Design
- Author photo: Chelsie Jensen Photography

To all who serve in the political sphere.

CONTENTS

Pursuing the Politicians   1

1. Arrested   3
2. Away   9
3. Aftermath   15
4. Action and Reaction   21
5. Hanging Out   29
6. Nighttime Confrontation   37
7. Morning Light   45
8. A Slow Start   49
9. Protesters Make a Turn   55
10. More Meetings   61
11. More Inspections   69
12. Food Fight   77
13. Capital Ideas   83
14. Sitting with the Sovereign   89
15. An Unexpected Visitor   97
16. Married at Last   103
17. Sunday Surprise   111
18. Emma's First Flight   117
19. Monday Morning Meetings   125
20. Emma's Vision   133
21. Getting Past Security   139
22. Homeward Bound   145
23. Airport Opportunities   149
24. Morning Stupor   155
25. Media Plans   159
26. Federal Agents   163
27. Released   169

28. Last Chance   173

Restoring the Repentant   177

About Peter DeHaan   185

Fiction Books by Peter DeHaan   187

PURSUING THE POLITICIANS

In a world just like ours . . . only different.

Your leaders have turned their backs on me and opposed my ways. I will turn my back on them and oppose their ways. They will be disgraced, and I will be exalted. -Prophecy 78.1

1

ARRESTED

Emma Barlow pulled out her phone to silence it when a text came in. It was from Michael Johnson, the principal at Riverside High, the school she had attended before becoming the High Priestess. *He's never texted me. Something's up.*

Emma read the text. "May the Sovereign bless you today at school."

Less than a week ago, he had warned her that the government might try to shut down their microschool. He also said he didn't dare text her, which would create a record that could be used against him. Since he texted her today, it must be important. Really important. Emma concluded that today was the day when it all might come down.

She sent a quick text alerting Hernandez, the chief of security. As an afterthought, she also texted Scarlett Steele, the reporter assigned to cover her and everything that happened on the Temple grounds. Once finished, Emma shoved her phone into the back pocket of her jeans.

Sitting in the classroom of her microschool, Emma waited for her teacher to arrive. To her left sat her bestie, Chloe. They were roommates during the week. To her right sat her boyfriend, Joshua. Their ten friends—her disciples—sat scattered behind them. Her puppy, Montgomery, hadn't gone to doggie daycare, so he snuggled in his favorite spot in the back corner.

Jennifer arrived to signal the beginning of school, yet most of the students had already begun their assignments. As for Emma, her algebra book lay open in front of her, but she couldn't focus. Instead of worrying about what might happen, she prayed instead, asking for the Sovereign's divine protection for her, her friends, and their microschool. Peace flooded her being.

With her focus restored, she began working through her algebra problems. But a commotion soon interrupted her. Alarmed, Emma turned around. There stood an uptight-looking woman wearing an ill-fitting business suit. Two police officers flanked her.

"May I help you?" Jennifer asked. Their teacher moved toward the unwelcome guests.

"We're here to observe your so-called school," the woman said. "I'm authorized by district headquarters and acting on behalf of the capital."

"You need to schedule your observations with me in advance." Jennifer moved closer to them. "Your presence is interrupting my students. I insist you leave immediately."

"Though we often extend the courtesy, we're not required to provide advance notice." The woman planted her fist on her hip and scowled. "The urgency of the situation required immediate action. We must protect the children."

Hernandez burst into the room, but one of the police officers held up his left hand while placing his right hand on his holstered sidearm. Hernandez halted his approach while his gaze darted around the room.

Emma stood and moved toward her teacher to confront the threat. "In the name of the Sovereign, I command you to leave."

The woman laughed. "I care nothing about the

Sovereign or your antiquated beliefs. Your idle threats mean nothing to me."

Emma edged up to Jennifer.

The other police officer stepped toward Emma while avoiding eye contact. "With all due respect, High Priestess," he said with a slight bow, "I will detain you if needed." He reached for Emma's shoulder to push her away from Jennifer.

A yipping Montgomery raced to the officer and nipped at his ankle. The guard swung his leg to kick the tiny puppy, but Montgomery was too fast.

"Leave my dog alone!" Emma lunged toward the officer, but Joshua's muscular arms pulled her back. He spun Emma away from the officer and stepped toward the uniformed man.

The officer glared at Joshua. "Do you want me to arrest you?"

"It wouldn't be the first time I was arrested for protecting Emma." Joshua stomped closer to the officer and glared back.

"I've seen enough of this circus," the stern woman stated. "There is no education occurring here. This is not a school. It's nothing more than a ruse to circumvent these children from receiving their legally mandated education." The woman jabbed her finger at Jennifer. "You're no teacher. You're nothing but a fraud."

Jennifer held her ground. "I suggest you familiarize yourself with how a microschool functions. Not only are these students excelling at their work, they're also ahead of where they should be at this point in the school year."

The woman shook her head. "You're only allowed to have ten students. I count thirteen. That puts you in violation."

"She's not our only teacher," Emma interjected. "We also have Elizabeth Butler here on staff."

The woman shook her head. "Not according to my records. And that's all that matters." She nodded to the police officer standing nearest her.

"Jennifer Russell," the man said, "I'm placing you under arrest."

2

AWAY

The two police officers handcuffed Jennifer and escorted her from the classroom. As they left, Hernandez advanced toward the woman. "You have no authority here." He jabbed a stern finger at her face. "Do you have a warrant? What are the charges?"

Unfazed, the woman held her ground. She looked up at Hernandez and laughed. "I can do whatever I want, and no one can stop me. Not you. Not the High Priestess. And not your delusional religion."

Hernandez crossed his arms and planted his feet on the floor, blocking her path to the closest exit. "You shouldn't even be here. I insist you release our teacher and leave at once."

With the woman's attention diverted, Emma backed away and snuck out the other door of the classroom. When Montgomery followed her, she extended her hand, palm out, to stop him. To her surprise, he plopped his rear on the floor and watched her leave.

As Emma rushed to reach the two policemen, she breathed a silent prayer. *Help me, Sovereign!*

Be nice and you'll achieve your goal, came the Sovereign's instructions implanted in Emma's mind.

Emma slowed her pace as she neared the officers. She exhaled deeply, expelling the tension from inside. She inhaled slowly and smiled. "Can we talk about what just happened?"

They stopped walking and the closest man turned toward Emma as she caught up to them. She walked around to face them and Jennifer.

"I'm sorry for kicking at your dog." The officer hung his head. "I knew better and shouldn't have done it. It's just that my frustration at being here got the better of me."

"You don't want to be here?"

The officer shook his head. So did his partner. "The plan from the beginning was to arrest her. But it was without merit and unjustified. We have nothing to charge her with."

The other officer spoke. "We'll hold her for twenty-four hours and then release her. So it will all work out."

"Or you can release her now. I imagine it will save you a bunch of paperwork." Emma grinned. "And it will keep Jennifer from spending the night in jail."

The men looked at each other.

Emma took a step forward and rested her hand on her teacher's shoulder. "Jennifer, under the Sovereign's power, I release you from your restraints."

Her handcuffs rattled to the ground.

Jennifer brought her hands in front of her and rubbed her wrists. "Much better."

The shocked police officers stared at Emma. The second man picked up the handcuffs and examined them. "I don't believe what I'm seeing."

Emma smiled. "You didn't release her. The Sovereign did. That puts you in the clear. May we go?"

The first officer shrugged. "I don't see why not. Please forgive us for our role in what just happened."

Emma guided Jennifer away from the shocked officers but then stopped and turned around to face them. She extended her arms, one palm facing each man. "I proclaim the Sovereign's blessings on you. May you find favor with your supervisor over what just happened. Amen."

The men received Emma's blessings and returned to their patrol car. As they drove away, Emma retreated to the school building, while Jennifer raced to get out of view.

As Emma got closer to the school, the woman rushed out.

Hernandez stomped after her. "I don't want to ever see you here again." He thrust a pointed finger at the retreating woman.

As the woman brushed past Emma, Jennifer ducked behind a clump of bushes. The woman didn't notice Jennifer diving out of sight. Instead, she made a beeline toward her car.

Emma didn't like that the woman had interrupted school and arrested Jennifer, but a holy indignation rose within her over how the woman had disrespected the Sovereign.

Is it okay if I show your power to her? Emma asked the Sovereign.

When the Sovereign didn't respond, Emma decided to do just that.

The woman jumped in her car, started it, and squealed the tires as she accelerated to leave.

Emma thrust her hand toward the car. It stopped with a jerk, and the engine stalled. The woman glared at Emma.

"This is a demonstration of the Sovereign's power," Emma proclaimed. "Never criticize my Lord or my faith again."

With eyes opened wide, the woman stared at Emma. "What did you do? Release me immediately."

"I didn't do anything. The Sovereign did. Never forget that."

The woman shook her fist. She started the car again and gripped the steering wheel. The engine raced, and the tires spun, but the car didn't move. Smoke billowed from the engine as the tires squealed.

As if locked in place, the car shook, straining to escape an unseen force. The more the engine roared, the more the car shuddered, but it didn't move—not one inch. It quaked as if about to shake apart.

"I demand that you release my car now!" the woman screamed.

You may do what she says, the Sovereign told Emma.

When Emma lowered her outstretched hand, the car lurched forward and careened into a light post in the parking lot. The airbag went off, and the engine stopped. Smoke wafted from the wreck. The woman slumped forward and didn't move.

"The Sovereign assures me she'll be okay," Emma told Hernandez, "but please call an ambulance . . . and a tow truck."

3

———

AFTERMATH

Hernandez left to check on the woman and call for help, and Emma's disciples rushed to her. Montgomery bounded up too.

"That was so amazing," Chloe said. "I recorded the entire thing."

"Me too," Lane added. "I also got everything in our classroom."

Jennifer hobbled up to the group, brushing grass and leaves from her clothes.

"Are you all right?" Emma asked their teacher.

Jennifer nodded. "Mostly, at least. I hurt my thigh a bit when I dove behind the bushes. But I couldn't risk letting that woman see me and rearrest me."

Joshua rushed up to Jennifer. "Does it hurt to walk? You can lean on me if it helps."

"I think I just need to walk it off," Jennifer said. "But as I do, I'll gladly take you up on your offer." She reached out and grabbed Joshua's extended arm. Together, they worked their way to the building and went inside.

Everyone but Emma followed. Ashley awaited her at the entrance. "That was intense," the young woman said. "And you were amazing!"

"Did you have a successful outing?" Emma asked.

Ashley nodded. "We got our marriage license, and we're ready. If it's not too much of a rush, can we get married this Saturday? I know it's only two days away, but there's not much we need to do to get ready."

"Works for me," Emma said. "But let me bring Frederick and Christopher in on this to make sure we do everything right. And Mark too. We also need the agreement for you to live in the High Priest's residence until you find a place of your own."

A dreamy smile grew on Ashley's face. "I can hardly wait to get married!" A slow sigh eased from her.

Emma smiled back. "Let me text the guys."

"And I'm ready to take Montgomery for the rest of the day." Ashley bent down and clipped his leash to his collar. "I hear he defended you and nearly got hurt."

"The Sovereign protected him." But then Emma wondered about what she said. *Does the Sovereign care for animals too?* Probably. They were, after all, part of creation.

As Ashley and Montgomery paraded away, Emma returned to her classroom. She paused at the doorway as Jennifer prayed. "Thank you, Lord, for protecting us and keeping us safe from everything that happened this morning. Please help us move beyond this ordeal and refocus on our studies. May we do so for your honor and glory and kingdom. Amen."

Emma finished her schoolwork about fifteen minutes before noon. She texted Fred, Christopher, and Mark that she was available to discuss Topher and Ashley's wedding. They already had their food when she reached the cafeteria. She quickly selected her lunch and joined them.

Fred held an official-looking document. "Lynn drafted a simple lease agreement to let Topher and Ashley live in the High Priest's residence for up to three months—but no more—as they look for a place to live. Topher signed it, and I'll get Ashley's signature after lunch."

Mark spoke next. "Emma, we all like your idea of conducting weddings as we read in the Holy Text. You have our full support."

"I have our wedding policy mostly drafted," Fred added. "It allows Temple employees to hold wedding ceremonies in the old sanctuary and have a celebration meal in the cafeteria at no cost. If anyone else wants to have their wedding here, there will be a fee. For all of them, we'll restrict weddings to Saturday afternoon or any weekday evening. But not Saturday night or anytime on Sunday. Our Sunday services take precedence."

"Is it rushing things to have the wedding this Saturday?" Emma asked. "Perhaps at 2:00?"

"I checked with the cafeteria staff, and they're good with it," Christopher said. "What we're still trying to work out is how they can prepare the food and watch the ceremony too. Everyone wants to be there. But not to worry, we'll figure something out."

"I'll text them the good news," Emma said.

Fred shook his head. "I'll handle that. A more pressing concern has arisen that you must know about."

Emma, Mark, and Christopher turned to Fred as the rest of the team joined them at the table.

Fred waited as everyone got settled. "I just received word that a Senate bill introduced today will restrict the High Priest to being male and over eighteen."

Emma gasped. "Can they do that?"

"Any Senator can introduce any bill he or she wants. The question is, will it pass? If it does, it will make it illegal for you to be High Priestess and block you from any leadership position here at the Temple. It also contains an ambiguous clause about reinstating prior leadership in the event of an opening. The speculation is that if the bill passes, the Prime Minister will pardon Barney Clark, which will open the door for his return."

Emma couldn't believe what she was hearing. "When I met with the Prime Minister last week, she asked if I'd work with her just like Barney did. I didn't know what she meant, but I turned her down just the same. That might be why she's out to get me and asked for someone to submit this bill. I think she wants me out so she and Barney can resume whatever scheme they were working on."

Mark turned to Fred. "What do you recommend we do to counter this and make sure the bill never passes?"

"I made some inquiries with trusted friends at the capital and am awaiting their input," Fred said.

Emma perked up. "Can I post a video asking people to respectfully contact their senators to oppose this bill?"

"Given the circumstances," Fred said, "I think that's a wise idea. And the sooner the better." Then he turned to Mark. "Will you draft an official response to this bill and have Lane post it on our website?"

"I'm already thinking about it," Mark said.

Fred stood. "On that note, let's adjourn our meeting so Emma and Mark can focus on getting the word out. If anyone has other ideas, let me know."

Everyone left but Emma. She had wanted to talk about the protesters who had showed up last Saturday. They'd been marching at the Temple's main entrance in opposition to the new policy about priest training. Emma expelled a frustrated sigh. *I guess that will need to wait.*

4

ACTION AND REACTION

Emma shuffled from the cafeteria as thoughts swirled in her mind. She paused before a picturesque maple tree to use as a background for her video. Emma shook the tension from her shoulders and smiled. She pressed the record icon on her phone.

"In case you haven't heard, a Senate bill was introduced today to block me from being High Priestess. If you disagree with this bill and don't want the government interfering with our faith, please contact your senator and ask that they oppose this bill. But be nice, because everything we do reflects the Sovereign. Thanks for your support."

Emma stopped the recording and posted the video online. Before she put her phone away, another idea came to her. She texted Scarlett. "If you're interested in discussing today's Senate bill, I'm available for an interview."

Emma slid her phone into the back pocket of her jeans and headed to the school building. She found Mrs. Butler in the second classroom. The teacher smiled when she saw Emma. "I'm about ready to receive our new class of priests on Monday. I'm so excited."

The news thrilled Emma, and her eyes twinkled. But she hadn't come for an update. "Did you hear about what happened this morning?"

Mrs. Butler looked down solemnly. "Lane showed me both videos."

"So you're aware there's a problem with your paperwork to teach at our microschool?"

"I already talked to Principal Johnson. He verified my paperwork was correctly filled out and on file. Plus, he contacted the district offices to let them know the investigator overlooked it. He also sent Jennifer a form that permits her to have more than ten students in class. It's a mere formality, and she's already submitted it. From a legal standpoint, we're ready—at least for teaching high schoolers."

"Great news!" Emma said. "That's one less

thing for me to worry about. Thanks for all you're doing. I really appreciate it."

Leaving Mrs. Butler to finish preparations for the Priest Academy, Emma headed to the front of the palace, which would give her a clear view of the entrance to the Temple grounds at the bottom of the hill. The protesters were still there. There seemed to be even more of them.

"Sovereign Lord, please give me insight about what to do."

As she waited for the Sovereign's instructions, Emma began counting. *Sixty-seven. That's definitely more than last week.*

The Sovereign's response formed in Emma's mind. *Some of them are wanted criminals. Also, they're being paid to protest. Follow the money.*

Thank you! Emma prayed in her spirit as she watched the Xtend News Network van turn into the Temple ground entrance and drive up the steep path. It stopped in front of the palace. Scarlett hopped out. "We were in the area and thought we'd stop by. When would be a good time for our interview?"

"How about now?"

"That works for us." Scarlett beamed. "Where do you suggest we conduct it?"

"There's a nice sitting room in the High Priest's residence. It will work nicely. I've not been there for weeks, but it should be ready for us to use."

Emma led the way. "How are your investigations going?"

The enthusiasm washed from Scarlett's face. "Aside from taping their protests and knowing where they're staying, I'm not making much progress."

"The Sovereign revealed to me that some protesters are wanted criminals," Emma said. "Let me see their pictures, and I'll point out who they are. Also, they're all being paid to protest. Follow the money."

"That will help me move forward," Scarlett said.

"What about your investigation into the Prime Minister's part in trying to shut down our school and threatening me?"

Scarlett looked away. "I'm not even sure where to start."

"Check with Frederick. He made some inquiries with his contacts at the capital and may have ideas for you. Also, Barney and the Prime Minister had some private way of communicating. Perhaps there's a trail on his work computer. It's still in my office. No one's touched it since he left. I'll let Frederick know it's okay for you to poke around. Ask Lane if you need technical help."

"I appreciate your insight."

When Emma showed Scarlett the sitting room in the High Priest's residence, she oohed when she saw the space. "This is perfect!"

The cameraman miked them both and cued Scarlett to begin.

"Scarlett Steele here with Xtend News Network. It's my privilege to bring you this exclusive interview with the High Priestess, Emma Barlow. Emma, the new Senate bill shocked me. It seems targeted specifically to remove you from the priesthood. What's your response?"

"I'm disappointed, but not surprised," Emma said. "I met with the Prime Minister last week. Without revealing details, let's just say that the meeting didn't go well. She threatened me."

"Were there any witnesses?"

Emma shook her head. "But her asking for a bill to bar me from being High Priestess seems to confirm it."

"The timing is certainly suspect," Scarlett said. "What can we do to oppose this misguided bill?"

"Everyone who doesn't want to see this legislation move forward should contact their senator and ask them to oppose it, but please be nice when you do. Senator Warren sponsored the bill. If you're in his district, let him know if you don't approve. You can call, email, or text. If everyone acts today, we can kill this bill before it goes any further."

"I hope everyone watching will do just that," Scarlett said. "But in a worst-case scenario, what will you do if the bill passes?"

"If I must choose, I will obey the Sovereign over this bill. I will remain High Priestess as long as it's the Sovereign's will. If I must break the law to do so, then I will be an outlaw."

"Regardless of what happens, you have my support. I suspect you also have the support of many others around the country. But if everyone contacts their senators today, hopefully we can stop this bill." Scarlett paused and looked at Emma. "If we may move onto another topic, I'd also like to talk about—"

"What are you doing here?" screamed a uniformed man who burst into the room.

The camera operator spun around to video the man.

"You must leave at once. If you refuse, I'll have you arrested—all three of you."

"On what grounds?" Emma asked.

"This space is quarantined, and we just condemned the entire palace as being unfit for human habitation."

Emma stood and stepped toward the man. "Why?"

"There's lead contamination in the High Priest's residence. You yourself confirmed it last week in your interview. To protect everyone, the entire palace is now quarantined."

"The lead contamination problem was minor and fixed last Friday," Emma said.

"It must first be tested to confirm that," the man said. "So far, that has not happened. Until it passes, you must not be in this building."

Fred scurried into the room, panting. He clutched a paper. "Yes, it has. Here are the test results. There is no sign of lead contamination." He handed the paper to the man.

The official snatched the paper and scowled at it. "This is not an officially requested test. It carries no weight with my department."

Fred glared at the man. "Environmental Testing Laboratories conducted the test. That's the same firm you contract with to do all your testing. Are you questioning their results?"

"I am not," the man stammered. "I wasn't aware of this . . . I haven't even put in the test request."

"Then that's on you," Fred said.

Scarlett stepped up to the official. "Does this mean you're admitting this is all your fault?" She thrust the microphone toward him.

The man looked at Scarlett and glanced at the camera. His hands trembled. "It seems . . . it seems a paperwork problem has occurred. I must investigate. Until then, you may use this facility on a provisional basis. But don't assume this is over." He backed away into the doorframe and winced. "I'll be back." He spun around and dashed from the room.

Emma edged up to Scarlett and whispered, "That should make for a good story. Feel free to hang out here, so you're ready to cover it when he returns."

5

HANGING OUT

That evening, Emma sat at the table in the cafeteria where she normally met with her team for lunch. But her team wasn't there. The ten new students for the priest school were. Montgomery snoozed at her feet.

Emma scanned the group. "Though this is an unofficial time to hang out, I'd like to officially welcome you to the inaugural class of our Priest Academy. No one else will ever be able to say they were first. You will. Being the first, your success will prepare future classes to be successful as well."

Emma took a sip of milk. "Tonight I'd like to spend some time getting to know each other as we eat dinner. I'll introduce each of you to the group. Then it will be your turn."

Emma started with Principal Johnson on her left. With him being a student here at the Temple, their roles were reversed. It would take Emma a while to get used to that. "This is Michael Johnson. He was the principal at Riverside High. But he feels he can have a bigger impact here as a priest. And I agree."

Emma looked to Michael's left. "Next is Jerry. He worked as a prison guard in Lakeview County and helped me free the prisoners. You might say that we battled evil together. He was the first one to talk to me about becoming a priest. He moved here just for that."

Emma continued around the circle. "I met Ethan for the first time last Saturday. He's a seminary grad, but they didn't study the Holy Text. That's why he's here—also because the Sovereign called him. Though most of his studies didn't prepare him for what priests do here, I'm sure he'll be happy to share anything he learned that might be helpful."

As Emma moved her attention to Olivia, she guarded what she shared. "Olivia went to college to be a counselor and hopes she can provide counseling services at the clinic. I sense we have an untapped need for that and know she can help."

Olivia cleared her throat. "What Emma didn't mention . . ." The woman dropped her head and looked down, "is that I made . . . I made some poor choices earlier in my life. I've been through extensive counseling to deal with it. Seeing how much it helped me made me want to help others. That's why I got my counseling degree and why I'm here. Emma helped me see that."

"Thanks, Olivia," Emma said. "Next, we have Zoe. I'm so excited to have her here. I see so much potential in her—so does the Sovereign. She has a background in food services and a desire to make an impact here. I'm sure she will."

Emma took another sip of milk. She really wanted to eat, like everyone else, but that would have to wait. She'd end up talking with food in her mouth. *That never works out well.* "The next five students in your class all have experience working here at the Temple. Victoria and Courtney both worked in our hospitality department."

"We were maids," Victoria interjected.

"Instead of making beds," Courtney added, "we want to make disciples for the Sovereign."

"And you will," Emma said. "Next, we have Justin and Rachel. They both come from the food services department. Justin worked in preparation

6

NIGHTTIME CONFRONTATION

Having received Mark's approval for Michael to spend mornings for the next two weeks at the high school, Emma shuffled off to her office in the palace.

She enjoyed having Chloe around as a roommate, but it involved some changes to her routine. Yes, they had fallen into a comfortable rhythm in the mornings. Chloe would get up first to shower and get ready for school. Then she'd make sure Emma was actually awake and getting up. As Emma got ready for the day, Chloe would study the Holy Text.

Yet evenings hadn't gone so well. Emma had retreated to her office in the palace to study the Holy Text each night. That was the only solution that allowed her to fully concentrate and not inconvenience Chloe. Though Emma willingly made this compromise, she struggled a bit to adjust.

Sitting at her office desk, Emma pulled out her copy of the Holy Text, opened her notebook, and lit the two candles. She was soon ready to study. Though she started late—later than she had wanted—she committed to studying for at least one hour.

At 10:30, a fatigued Emma shuffled to her room in the priests' quarters. Montgomery, seeming to sense her melancholy mood, trotted dutifully at her side. Emma opened the door to her darkened quarters. A sleeping Chloe emitted a barely discernible breath.

Emma stepped forward and stubbed her toe on something. It was Chloe's shoe. Emma kicked it aside, hurting her toe a second time. Two more steps and Emma encountered the other shoe. When it came to housekeeping, Chloe was a total slob, something Emma hadn't realized until now.

To avoid any more unpleasant surprises, Emma inched her way to her dresser. But as she reached to open the top drawer, she encountered a pair of Chloe's jeans thrown on top of it. In the dark, Emma folded the jeans the best she could and laid them on the dresser. With pajamas in hand, Emma inched to the bathroom, where she got ready for the night.

Soon she slipped into bed. Montgomery jumped up and burrowed between the two of them. At least he had no trouble adjusting to Chloe's presence.

Emma closed her eyes, intending to thank the Sovereign for her day and asking for peaceful rest, but she fell asleep before her mind formed a single word.

In the middle of the night, a force rammed into Emma's stomach, and she doubled over. She screamed in pain. Yet her room in the priests' quarters was at peace. Emma's spirit rushed into the spiritual realm. A black force was upon her—jet black. It was the spirit of the Prime Minister. Roused from her slumber, Emma's white light was dim in this dark domain of evil.

Emma also sensed the Prime Minister was more powerful than the formidable Barney Clark. Though she had defeated him, could she defeat the Prime Minister?

Pinned down, Emma couldn't shoot bolts of light or throw supernatural projectiles at the Prime

Minister's spirit. Quoting Scripture was her only recourse, for evil hates the light of the Holy Text. "When danger surrounds you, the Sovereign will light your path, push back the darkness, and drive evil away," Emma cried out in her spirit. Her white light grew brighter.

The black orb shook, lessening for a moment its grab on Emma's spirit.

"The Sovereign demands justice," Emma proclaimed. "The unjust will perish—"

A heavy blow to Emma's spirit stopped her from speaking further truth. As if a hand clamped over her mouth, Emma could say no more. Trapped and defenseless, her spirit trembled. Though she could plead with the Sovereign to defend her, Emma sensed that, just as with Barney Clark, this battle was hers to fight and to win—or to lose.

Evil minion demons darted about, shrieking with delight and jeering at her with glee.

The Prime Minister also mocked her. "What do you have to say for yourself, missy? You're not as powerful as you thought. My beloved Bernard was weak for not being able to defeat you. I will prevail where he failed."

Emma's light dimmed.

"Leave her alone!" The sound came from a lime

green light in the distance. It moved closer. "In the name of the Sovereign, I command you to leave." It was Chloe. Chloe had entered the spiritual realm to help Emma. Chloe's essence zoomed toward them, on a collision course with the Prime Minister.

This distracted the Prime Minister just long enough for Emma to free herself from the evil woman's grasp. "The Sovereign demands justice," Emma called out. "The unjust will perish along with their folly."

The Prime Minister turned back toward Emma. This diverted her attention from the charging Chloe, who rammed into her with a sickening thud. The Prime Minister shot in one direction and Chloe bounced in another. The Prime Minister's glossy black dimmed, while Chloe's lime green light disappeared altogether.

This gave Emma time to recover. She shot forth three rapid bolts of light, each one hitting the Prime Minister. She followed with a projectile. Though it moved slower, it was also more powerful. Much more. The dazed Prime Minister couldn't react in time as the projectile scored a direct hit.

The Prime Minister's demon minions rushed to her aid. Many gave her what little power they had, each one recharging her a bit to make her stronger.

Others formed a shield before her, while the rest bolstered her from behind.

Emma shot forth a barrage of light, but the demon army protected the Prime Minister. She heckled Emma and told her to try harder. Emma followed with the biggest projectile she could muster, but it left her weak. The demons absorbed its blow, with many of them blipping into oblivion. Yet the Prime Minister remained untouched.

"Approach the Sovereign with a pure heart and live; those with selfish intent will perish—be it in body or in spirit." This was the verse that had inflicted the most damage on Barney Clark, yet it only made the Prime Minister laugh. "You forget that I care nothing for your silly little religion. It makes you weak. I am strong."

Nearly spent, Emma wondered how much longer she could continue to fight.

But two orbs appeared in the distance. One was Chloe's lime green aura. The other was blue. It was Joshua! Together, the pair of lights flew toward the Prime Minister. Emma supernaturally shared a plan with them. As they neared the Prime Minister, Chloe circled to the left as Joshua went right.

As Emma shot forth another barrage of lightning bolts, Chloe emitted a rapid-fire series of sound waves that pulsed toward the Prime Minister like storm waves crashing upon the shore.

Joshua's attack surprised Emma even more. She could best compare it to a booming cannon. It shot forth with both the speed of her bolts of light and with the power of her projectiles.

Their salvos reached the Prime Minister at the same time. Many of her demon minions zapped into nothingness. The rest of them scurried away.

Emma's white light grew brighter, bolstered by Joshua's blue and Chloe's green. The Prime Minister's glossy black sheen faded further.

Emma sought to finish her. "Approach the Sovereign with a pure heart and live; those with selfish intent will perish—be it in body or in spirit."

As she repeated the verse a second time, Joshua and Chloe joined her. "Approach the Sovereign with a pure heart and live; those with selfish intent will perish—be it in body or in spirit."

The Prime Minister's blackness paled to nothing and then disappeared.

Hundreds of angels rushed forward to celebrate the glorious victory. They had been there the whole time, cheering on Emma, Chloe, and Joshua.

Though the war against the Prime Minister was far from over, Emma had won the first battle.

7

MORNING LIGHT

Emma's eyes popped open with a start. She sat up in bed, fully alert, which was quite surprising given that it wasn't yet morning.

Sitting next to her, Chloe laid a gentle hand on Emma's shoulder. "You had me worried, girlfriend."

"Thanks for rescuing me," Emma said. "The Prime Minister's spirit caught me off guard and had me pinned. I couldn't do anything. If you hadn't shown up when you did, she would've finished me for good."

"I didn't do anything," Chloe said.

"You distracted her long enough for me to get

free. You saved me. Did the Sovereign tell you I needed help?"

Chloe shook her head. "You screamed in your sleep. I thought you were having a nightmare and tried to wake you, but I couldn't. Then you began thrashing about, and I wondered if it was something happening in the spiritual realm. I entered it, just like you taught me."

"So glad you did," Emma said.

"I saw you were in trouble, but I didn't know what to do. All I could think of was to ram her as hard as I could. So I did."

"That was exactly what I needed. Did it hurt? Are you okay?"

"My shoulder's throbbing. A lot." Chloe rubbed her joint as she tried to rotate it. "Why?"

"What happens in the spiritual realm affects our physical bodies," Emma explained. "You should go to the clinic."

"What about the Prime Minister? Is she dead? Did we kill her?"

"I don't think so," Emma said, "but I imagine she's not feeling so well right now."

Emma's phone rang. It was Joshua. She answered. "You're on speaker. You all right?"

"I'm fine," Joshua said. "But what about you

and Chloe? I fought from afar. You two were in the middle of things."

"Chloe's shoulder hurts. And my stomach is sore, but I feel okay. Thanks for checking. And thanks for rescuing me—again!"

"That's what boyfriends do," Joshua said. "I'm so glad Chloe called me."

"What? Chloe called you?" Emma asked. "In the middle of the night?"

"Actually, she texted me to call her," Joshua said. "She let me know what was happening, and we formed a plan. You know the rest."

Emma thanked Joshua again for his help and said good night.

"Actually, it's almost morning," Joshua said. "Rise and shine!" He disconnected before Emma could give him a sarcastic retort.

"I'm going to get an early start on my day," Chloe said.

"And I'm going back to sleep," Emma countered. She lay down and rolled over. Montgomery nestled next to her.

The next thing Emma knew, someone was shaking her shoulder. "Emma, you need to get up." The voice sounded familiar.

Emma groaned. "My alarm hasn't even gone

off yet, Mom."

"It's gone off three times." But the voice wasn't her mom's, it was Chloe's. "If you don't get up now, you're going to miss breakfast."

"Let me know when you're done with your shower."

"I had my shower, got ready for school, and read the Holy Text. You must get up. Now!" Chloe jerked the covers off Emma and tossed them aside, burying Montgomery. He wiggled forth and stuck his head out.

"Wake her up, Montgomery!" Chloe commanded.

The puppy leapt forward and gave Emma's cheek an enthusiastic lick.

"Okay. Okay." Emma flailed her arms. "I'm getting up. Both of you, stop harassing me."

8

A SLOW START

Emma ate breakfast with the priests as usual. Chloe ate breakfast with her grandpa, something they had started just this week. Each morning, Gabe got up early so they could spend time together.

Although still groggy from the interruption to her sleep, Emma corralled her thoughts enough to ask the priests a question. "I'd like to open a satellite location in the capital for a Sunday service to minister to the politicians. We need to influence them for the Sovereign."

Fred perked up. "A live service or remote?"

"I'm thinking remote. No need to duplicate what we're already doing." Emma scanned the group to gauge their interest. "Our focus there should be on making connections before and after the service—and throughout the week. Let Mark know if you want to move there and help. We can talk more about it later."

A lively discussion followed, and Emma sensed some priests were interested. She wanted to hear what they had to say, but a text from Scarlett ended that. Emma excused herself.

"Any idea what Barney's computer password might be?" Scarlett had written.

Emma grinned. "Try Montgomery," she texted back.

"Seriously? His dog's name?"

"Montgomery Philanthropy Fund is also the name of the shell company he used to launder the money he stole from us."

"Montgomery works! You're brilliant!"

"The Sovereign revealed it to me!"

Emma returned to the priests' table, but their discussion was over and most had left. She did too. She trudged toward school, while Chloe bounced along at her side. It was that way most every morning.

"I don't understand," Chloe said. "Why weren't you protected last night when you were sleeping?

How was the Prime Minister's spirit able to attack you so easily?"

Emma let out a repentant sigh. She knew the answer, but she kept quiet.

"We were safe when I spent the night with you in the High Priest's residence," Chloe said. "Why weren't we safe last night?"

"Because I messed up. We had claimed the High Priest's residence as a sanctified place with no room for evil. I also did that when I moved into the lower level of the priests' quarters. But I forgot to do it when I moved upstairs."

"Should we do it now?" Chloe asked.

"No need. Already did. We're good from now on."

Chloe rubbed her shoulder for the fourth time that morning. "Why don't you just declare the entire Temple grounds as a sanctified place with no room for evil? That covers everything."

"It's a big space," Emma said. "I doubt I can do it."

"But didn't you and Angie do something like that at the prison when you freed the prisoners?"

"Good point."

"How about you, me, and Joshua do it together? You take the lead, and we'll support you."

"Let me think about it."

They dropped off Montgomery at Ashley's salon. "No offense, Emma, but you don't look so good," Ashley said. "Are those bruises on your wrists?"

Emma inspected her forearms. Both had blotchy gray welts. She rubbed one and then the other. It must be from when the Prime Minister had restrained her in the spiritual realm. Emma's stomach wasn't the only casualty of their supernatural confrontation.

Before Emma could answer, Ashley's gaze darted to Chloe massaging her shoulder. "What's wrong with you?"

"We had a rough night in the spiritual realm," Emma said. "But don't worry, we'll be all right."

"When you have time, maybe you could tell me about it," Ashley said. "There's so much about the spiritual realm I don't understand."

"Let's do it next week after your wedding," Emma said. "Speaking of your wedding, I have a question."

"It's only a day away." A dreamy contentment fell over Ashley. "What's your question?"

"I like that we'll have the ceremony follow the Holy Text," Emma said. "From now on, I want all our weddings here to follow that. What would you think if Scarlett did a writeup of the ceremony to post online? No videos. No pictures. And no names. I just want her to describe the ceremony as an example for others to follow."

"I like that," Ashley said. "Let me check with Topher. I'll let you know."

Emma bent to ruffle the hair on Montgomery's head. "You be a good boy for Auntie Ashley. See you tonight." He darted to his doggie bed in the corner.

Emma and Chloe left the salon and headed toward school.

Chloe slowed her pace. She let out a deliberate breath and glanced at Emma. "Do you miss your family? It's not even been a week, and I miss Dad terribly. Not that I'm complaining about rooming with you. You're great. But still . . ."

"It was hard for me at first," Emma said, "but I'm so busy I scarcely have time to think about it. I see Dad here every day during the week, and I call or email Mom each night. I sometimes text the sibs too. Plus, we all eat lunch here together each Sunday after the service and hang out."

"I thought I'd have a lot of time to spend with Grandpa here during the week, but it's not as much as I thought. He and Dad are getting along great. I'm happy to give them space, but I wish I could be part of it. I can't wait to go home this weekend."

"Where will you sleep?"

"I gave Grandpa my room, so I'll sleep on the couch—assuming he lets me. He can be a bit stubborn when it comes to his principles."

"Surely there must be a solution. Let's pray about it."

When they finished praying, Chloe rubbed her shoulder again. A moan leaked from her lips.

"Let's go to the clinic and get you checked out before school," Emma said.

"Grandpa prayed for my healing. That helped a lot, but not completely. I took something for the pain after breakfast. It just needs time to kick in," Chloe said.

"Do you mean time for Gabe's prayer to kick in or the medicine?"

"Either is fine with me. And the sooner the better."

"If it's not better by lunch, I'll drag you to the clinic," Emma said.

9

PROTESTERS MAKE A TURN

By the time school started, Emma had finally woken up and was fully alert. She plunged into her assignments with enthusiasm and cranked through them.

Midmorning, the Sovereign interrupted her studies, implanting a warning in Emma's mind. Though silent, it was as clear—and as imperative—as if someone stood next to her and spoke aloud. *The protesters are about to charge the hill and are riled up to riot. Go stop their rebellion.*

Emma looked at Jennifer, cleared her throat, and gestured with her hand. "I need to leave. Be back soon."

Surprise blanketed Jennifer's face and concern shone in her eyes as Emma scurried away.

As fast as she could make her legs move, Emma raced toward the top of the main entrance to the Temple grounds. She watched in horror as the protesters, now nearly one hundred strong, stopped their march, tossed their signs aside with a roar, and streamed up the hill.

Their peaceful protest was turning physical. Possibly violent.

Though they had less distance to cover, Emma moved on level ground, while they had a steep hill to ascend. From painful experience, Emma knew it was a muscle-cramping, lung-throbbing climb. She could keep up her pace, but they wouldn't.

Emma reached the top of the drive before any of the protesters made it halfway there. *Halt their advance,* came the Sovereign's instructions.

Emma held out both hands and called out, "I declare this to be a sanctified place with no room for evil."

They stopped their arduous climb and stared up at her.

"You must leave." Emma lowered her right hand and gave a dismissive backward flip to the protesters. Most spun around and scurried down the hill. In their haste, a few tumbled. Emma prayed they'd be okay. A few picketers remained frozen for a time, but they soon retreated.

When the protesters reached the bottom of the hill, they didn't pick up their signs to resume their protest. They continued fleeing.

Their leader had remained at the bottom of the drive this entire time. He held up his hands to stop their withdrawal, but they continued down the road, scurrying away as if being chased by a swarm of bees. He screamed for them to come back. They did not. Soon they were out of sight.

Well done, came the Sovereign's affirmation. *Though they'll be back, they won't attack again.*

That's when Emma recognized she wasn't alone. Joshua had edged up on her right and Chloe on her left. That's when she realized they had joined her in her prayer to sanctify the space, to banish all evil.

Emma grabbed both of their hands. "Join with me in the spiritual realm. Don't let go." As a unit, they moved into the supernatural. Their spirits shone brightly, with Emma's the brightest. The demons fluttering about in mayhem scurried to the distance, while angels danced for joy around them.

"We declare the entire Temple grounds to be a

safe place," Emma cried out in her spirit. "From now on and forevermore, it will be a sanctuary for the Sovereign's followers. I banish all evil from these grounds forevermore and sanctify it for all time."

The demons skirted even further away as angels formed a protective hedge around the Temple grounds. With swords drawn, these supernatural beings sang their praises to the Sovereign.

When the trio returned to their physical reality, a shocked Scarlett edged up to them. She held a small video camera. "I got everything. It's a good thing, too, else I wouldn't believe what I just saw."

"You only saw what happened in our physical world," Emma said. "What happened in the supernatural realm was even more amazing."

"I can't even imagine." Scarlett shook her head.

Emma glanced at her two friends. "Thanks for everything. Better head back to class. I'll be there soon." She turned to face Scarlett. "I'll be interested to see what you do with your footage."

"So will I!" Scarlett said. "Did you hear about the Prime Minister?"

Emma shook her head.

"She was rushed by ambulance to the hospital early this morning," Scarlett said. "One unconfirmed source said she was in serious condition, but another insisted she's just there for observation."

"Interesting." Emma wondered if she should say more, but worried Scarlett wasn't ready to hear.

"The official statement from the Prime Minister's office is that she suffered a bit of dehydration because of a mild case of stomach flu last night. She's at the hospital as a mere precaution. They expect her to resume normal duties on Saturday."

"What else do you know?"

"There's a blurry picture of her online," Scarlett said. "It shows her on a stretcher, with one eye swollen shut and the rest of her face bruised and mottled. One of her arms and both legs are wrapped. Some claim it's fake and others insist it's real."

"What are people posting?"

Scarlett laughed. "Everything imaginable. Some speculate a heart attack or stroke. Others suggested a beating during a break-in or mugging. One blogger is sure it was an assassination attempt."

Emma rubbed her chin. "But what do you think?"

Scarlett lowered her voice, even though no one

else was around. "I think it's supernatural. That the Sovereign is punishing the Prime Minister for opposing you." Scarlett paused as she peered into Emma's eyes. "Am I right?"

"You're not far from the truth," Emma said, "but don't tell anyone."

10

———

MORE MEETINGS

Despite the morning's distraction, Emma, Chloe, and Joshua completed their day's schoolwork before lunch. The trio headed to the cafeteria.

Lane ran to catch them. "Scarlett found links to an email portal that she thinks Barney and the Prime Minister might have used to communicate, but she can't log in. Any ideas?"

Emma slowly shook her head, but then the Sovereign gave her supernatural insight. She laughed. "Try *Emma*."

Everyone stared at her. "Why would he use your name?" Lane asked. "He probably set up the account before he even knew you."

"There's more to it, but the Sovereign hasn't

revealed that to me. All I sense is that *Emma* has a special meaning to him."

Lane shrugged. "I'll try it." He jogged to the palace, leaving Emma, Chloe, and Joshua to head to lunch.

"How's your shoulder?" Joshua asked Chloe.

"It's back to normal." Chloe rotated her shoulder. "It couldn't feel better."

"Was it healing prayer or pain medicine?" Emma asked.

"I'm not sure," Chloe said. "Though I thought I needed it this morning, I wished I hadn't taken the pain meds and just relied on Grandpa's healing prayer. Then I'd know for sure." She turned to Emma. "What about your stomach and wrists?"

"Everything's fine," Emma said. "The Sovereign answered my prayers for healing. Even the bruises are gone." She held out her forearms and rotated them for Chloe and Joshua to see.

After getting their food from the cafeteria line, Joshua and Chloe walked to their usual table, where the rest of Emma's disciples would join them. Emma headed to her regular spot with her team for their working lunch. As she sat in her chair, she noticed the ten Priest Academy students at a third table. Their animated discussion suggested their morning went well.

Emma's team soon arrived.

Aurora, their architect, joined them and gave an update about the progress on building the new welcome center. Then she outlined the timetable for the other renovations. She ended by thanking everyone for giving her an office and a place to stay on the Temple grounds so she could maximize her impact and move things forward as quickly as possible.

When she excused herself to return to work, Mark spoke. "We have five priests interested in moving to the capital to open our site there. One of them is Frederick."

"With Emma's approval, of course," Fred said.

"You have my blessing," Emma responded. "The Sovereign told me to prepare for you to leave. I hoped it wouldn't be for a long time, but I accept that it could be soon."

"That will leave a critical position open," Mark said. "Do you have plans to fill it?"

"I do!" Emma said. "I recommend Christopher become our new executive administrator."

"But he doesn't have any experience for that role," Fred said.

"He didn't have experience for his present position, either," Emma said, "but he's doing a great job at it. I'm sure that will continue."

"That just creates another opening," Fred countered.

"I recommend Susie replace him as human resources director," Emma said.

Fred groaned. "Then we'll need a new office manager at the clinic."

"Natalie wants to work there," Emma said. "She hopes to become the office manager."

"She's only fifteen," Fred snapped.

"So am I," Emma shot back. "She has a mentor to guide her, Susie can support her, and my dad understands fifteen-year-old girls. We can make it work."

Fred stroked his beard. "I suppose so."

Emma turned to Mark. "Can you and I meet with the five priests who want to move to the capital? Will 4:00 work?"

Mark nodded.

Emma stood and blessed her team for the rest of their day. Then she excused herself and headed to where the Priest Academy students sat. "I sense your day is off to a good start," Emma said. "Though I'd like to hear about it, that will have to wait. I understand Jerry has an update for me." Emma looked at Jerry and gestured with her arm so they could leave to talk.

Jerry didn't move. "They already know about the situation. Once you released all the prisoners from jail, the prison authority laid off all the staff and announced the decommissioning of the facility. They can't have a secret prison in Lakeview County, since everyone now knows where it is."

"Are many people affected?" Emma asked.

"Far too many," Jerry answered. "The prison system was the second largest employer in the county. Their closure is devastating the local economy."

"What can we do?" Emma asked.

Jerry shrugged. "I hoped you would have ideas."

"I've been very concerned about our nation's prison system," Michael interrupted. "Before I came here to be a priest, I was considering resigning my position as high school principal to become a prison warden. I'm sure I could make a difference."

"What do you have in mind?" Emma asked.

"I'm still mulling over the details," Michael said, "but basically to repurpose that facility to be a training center and help prisoners prepare to re-enter society productively. This should help keep them from being re-incarcerated. I also think it should have a spiritual component."

"I like your thinking," Emma said. "Once you figure it out, will you write up your plan?"

"Maybe we can also open a satellite location there for Sunday services," Jerry suggested. "The need in the community is great."

"Do you mean a service at the prison?"

"Maybe." Jerry frowned. "Or perhaps we can rent the high school auditorium on Sundays. That's the best way to reach the entire community."

"I'm not sure about starting two satellite locations at the same time," Emma said. "But if there's an opportunity, I don't want to miss it."

Emma excused herself to make her 1:00 meeting with Scarlett back at her office.

"As you requested, I have pictures of all the protesters that I pulled from my videos," Scarlett said. "Lane printed them." She spread out four sheets of paper, each one—except for the last—with twenty-five pictures per page. "What do you plan on doing with them?"

"Once Hernandez arrives," Emma explained, "I'll share important background on some of them, as revealed by the Sovereign."

"I'm here," came Hernandez's panting voice from behind them.

"First, I'll point out all the protesters who have open arrest warrants for them or are being sought for questioning." As Emma pointed to the pictures of nine men, Hernandez put a check mark by each portrait.

"Here are twelve who are illegal aliens." Hernandez put the letter A on each one of their pictures.

"These three are here on expired student visas." Hernandez marked them with an S.

"And four are past due on alimony or child support," Emma announced. "Since they're being paid to protest, they need to pay what they owe their families."

Hernandez put a D on their pictures. "D for deadbeat," he explained. "I'll get this to my contact at the police station right away. Assuming it checks out, she'll be excited to have it. And I'll give you two all the credit."

"The credit goes to Scarlett for the pictures and the Sovereign for supernatural insight. Please leave me out of it."

"That may be challenging," Hernandez said. "But I'll do my best."

Emma pointed to one more picture. "This man is key."

"What did he do?" Scarlett asked.

"He's the one most likely to give you the information you need to expose their operation and find out who's behind it."

11

MORE INSPECTIONS

Emma left Scarlett and Hernandez in her office as she hurried to make her regular 2:00 meeting with the priests to talk about the Holy Text. Emma's trek to her meeting, however, was interrupted when a caravan of official-looking cars sped onto the Temple grounds. They parked in front of the new auditorium.

Emma sent Hernandez a quick text: "Help!" Then she remembered that prayer was her better option. *Help!*

The man in the lead car jumped out. He was the official from yesterday who had tried to condemn the palace as unfit for human habitation. He had threatened to come back. Now he had.

Pointing toward the various buildings, he directed his charges where to go. Each one scurried toward his assigned target.

Worried, Emma approached the man. Though concerned, she didn't want to appear confrontational. Emma smiled. "Hi!" She waved. "I didn't expect to see you so soon." She extended her hand to him, but he ignored it.

"We've received numerous complaints about your facility—serious ones, I might add," he said. "I'm charged with investigating them immediately."

Hernandez rushed up. "Are they from reputable sources?"

"That doesn't concern you," the man said. He looked at his clipboard. "We're inspecting the Temple, the construction of your new welcome center, both sanctuaries, your school, and your dorms. The health inspector will arrive shortly to go over your cafeteria with a fine-tooth comb."

Fred wheezed up. "We hold ourselves to the highest standards. Our facilities are in excellent shape."

"I'll be the judge of that," the man said.

Scarlett stood behind Fred, letting his portly frame hide her. She slowly raised her portable video camera and aimed it over his right shoulder. Its red light lit, but the official didn't notice.

That's when Aurora walked up and distracted the man. "Hi, I'm Aurora Blake. I'm the architect who designed the welcome center." She smiled at him. "I'm also serving as the construction manager and overseeing all the renovations here. I can assure you that everything is being done according to best practices and meets all legal requirements." Aurora extended her hand.

The man didn't shake her hand either. "Forgive me for not taking your word on this. I don't base my decisions on promises. I seek facts."

An inspector raced out of the new auditorium. He waved a paper in the air. "I found a problem and can confirm." He handed his findings to his leader.

The man looked at it and glared, the hint of a smile leaking from the corner of his lips. He pointed to the auditorium. "Effective immediately, that building is condemned."

Another inspector ran up from the construction site of the new welcome center. "I found a serious violation, and we must shut it down." He handed his findings to the lead inspector.

"Condemned! All work must cease immediately. I'm shutting down construction until further notice."

A line of breathless inspectors formed. Each one shared his findings with the lead inspector. Each time, he gleefully proclaimed, "Condemned!"

After submitting their individual reports, each man rushed to his car and sped away.

"What are the reasons?" Aurora asked. "The standard practice is to alert project management of any minor infractions to give them time to make corrections."

The man scowled at her. "This is anything but a standard situation. Lives are at stake."

"Let's work together to find a solution," Emma said. "What are your concerns?"

"That's no worry of yours, High Priestess." The man gave her a slight bow.

"This is outrageous!" Hernandez grabbed the papers from the man and handed them to Aurora.

"Seriously? You're shutting down construction because you saw a nail on the ground?" Aurora questioned. "That's common during construction. We'll address it all in the final cleanup phase."

"It presents a clear hazard to the public should they walk in the construction zone."

Aurora paged through the other reports. "I can't believe what I'm reading. You're condemning us for a leaky faucet, a janitor's mop pail without a warning sign, and broken glass. But the picture is of a small one-inch crack in a room that's closed to use. The dorm rooms have been shut down for years, and we are preparing to renovate them completely."

Hernandez had been peering over Aurora's shoulder. "Each one of these complaints comes from Barney Clark," Hernandez said. "Do you realize he's in prison on multiple serious charges against the High Priestess and our Temple operations? And the dates he filed his complaints are after his arrest. Surely, this is nothing more than a personal vendetta on his part."

Emma stepped forward. "I sense you're a good and honorable man," she said to the inspector. "This isn't who you are. What can we do to fix things?"

"I have my orders," the man said. He grabbed the papers back from Aurora. "This is official documentation that you shouldn't be privy to."

"What can we do to remedy this situation and not escalate things any further?" Fred asked.

The man glanced at Fred for the first time and

noticed Scarlett standing behind him with her camera. He held out his hand to block her shot. "I demand you stop recording immediately."

"We're streaming live," Scarlett said as she repositioned herself for a better shot.

"You have no business to record our work. You shouldn't even be here."

"I invited her," Emma said. "I gave her permission to go wherever she wants on the Temple grounds and report on anything she wishes."

Scarlett edged up to the inspector. "What do you have to say about your actions today? I'll give you this opportunity to explain yourself."

"I-I'm just following orders," the man stammered. "It comes from far above my pay grade."

"Who's your boss?" Scarlett asked. "I'd like to hear what he or she has to say about this."

"Please don't get him involved," the man said. "He was just doing what he was told to do as well. My understanding is that our orders came from the capital."

"Do you want to be known for following orders or for doing what is right?" Emma asked.

The man hung his head. Gripping the papers at the top, he held them up between his left and right hand. He tore the entire group in half, ripping them from top to bottom. "I'd rather do what's right. If that costs me my job, then so be it." He handed his shredded reports to Emma and walked away.

As he drove off, another official-looking car arrived. It was the health inspector.

FOOD FIGHT

Scarlett panned her camera to the cafeteria. "Our coverage of the events on the Temple grounds continues," she narrated to her audience. "The health inspector has just arrived. The building inspector had warned us this would happen. Let's see what he wants. We shouldn't jump to conclusions, but I wonder if the unjustified governmental assault against our faith continues."

Emma had already headed toward the cafeteria, and Scarlett hustled to catch up. Fred and Hernandez followed close behind.

Scarlett—not used to lugging a camera, even a small one—panted as she labored forward. Reaching the surprised inspector, Emma spoke, to give Scarlett time to catch her breath. "The building inspector has just left and told us to expect you. In the end, he didn't cite us for anything. I hope you'll reach the same conclusion."

"You were just here two days ago," Fred protested. "You gave us a perfect score for the second time in a row. I understand that's quite rare, and we're proud of our achievement."

"We received a serious allegation that demanded we re-examine your entire facility," the flustered inspector said.

"If it came from Barney Clark, I suggest you discount it," Hernandez said.

The man looked at his paperwork and grimaced.

"Are you aware he's been charged for attempted murder—among other things," Hernandez continued. "He's being held without bail for trying to poison the High Priestess through her food, so any allegations he might have about our cafeteria practices are certainly suspect."

"Stop recording," the health inspector hissed at Scarlett.

"We're streaming live," Scarlett said. "Please share with us the nature of these allegations and who they came from."

"That information is not for public knowledge."

He held up his hand. "Record if you must, but do so from a distance. You need to allow me to conduct my work without any interference. This applies to both cafeteria staff and media."

As the man walked toward the building's main entrance, Hernandez called out more information. "Barney Clark's been incarcerated for the past two weeks. If his complaint arrived since then, it was from within the prison and can't be based on first-hand knowledge. It's speculation at best."

The food inspector looked down at his paper-work as he walked. Shrugging his shoulders, he entered the cafeteria, and the doors swung shut behind him.

Scarlett continued to point her camera at the cafeteria's entrance, where the inspector had just disappeared. She recapped all that had happened for her audience, starting with the building inspector and concluding with the arrival of the health inspector. "With this as our background, perhaps we can get some comments from the High Priestess."

"Certainly," Emma said. She had but a second to prepare as Scarlett panned toward her.

"We know Barney Clark was behind the complaints that prompted the multiple building inspections," Scarlett said. "Though we can't state conclusively that he also filed the complaint against the cafeteria, we can't help but wonder. What do you think?"

"I don't want to speculate," Emma answered. "The Sovereign gives us grace and mercy. We should do the same for others."

"That's most generous, especially since he's been accused of poisoning you," Scarlett said. "If he tried to kill you, does he still deserve mercy?"

"We'll let the courts decide," Emma said. "I'm more concerned about his spiritual condition. Despite how he treated me, I pray he'll one day repent of his sins and be restored into a right relationship with the Sovereign."

"Are you talking about the afterlife?" Scarlett asked.

"Where he spends the rest of his life here on earth doesn't matter nearly as much as where he spends eternity."

The inspector approached Emma. He hadn't even been gone for a minute. He was no longer flustered and had a penitent look on his face. "Please forgive my impromptu arrival. I can confirm the complaint is baseless and without merit. I found no infractions."

As the health inspector walked away, Scarlett followed him with her camera. "What was the complaint?"

He continued walking.

"What exactly were you looking for?"

He shook his head.

"Did your orders come from the capital?"

He spun around and hissed, "I never said that!"

CAPITAL IDEAS

s Scarlett wrapped up her live feed, the inspector walked away and left in his car.

"I'm glad that's over," Emma said.

"It certainly could've gone a lot worse," Fred replied.

"The Sovereign granted us favor," Emma said.

As Aurora and Hernandez returned to their work, Scarlett carefully sat her camera on the ground and rubbed her shoulder. "Though it's supposed to be lightweight, it certainly gets heavy after a while."

Emma extended her hand toward the reporter. "May I?"

Scarlett cocked her head and gave Emma an inquisitive glance. "Um . . . I guess so."

Emma laid her hand on the reporter's shoulder. "I proclaim the Sovereign's healing on you. May the pain leave, full use return, and you not suffer any side effects."

Scarlett flexed her shoulder. "I can't believe it! You healed me!"

"The Sovereign healed you," Emma corrected. "And yes, you can believe it."

"Thank you!" Scarlett grinned. "Both of you."

"Any progress on Barney's email account?" Emma asked.

"We could log in, but he never sent any emails. There's one long message in draft mode, but there's something strange about how it's worded. It's like two people wrote it to each other, as if having a conversation. When I left, Lane said he had an idea he wanted to check into, but I don't hold out much hope. It looks like a dead end."

"Stay with it," Emma said. "I'm sure it will lead to something."

Before Scarlett could answer, Emma's phone chirped. "Frederick and I have a 4:00 meeting. May the Sovereign bless your investigation."

As Scarlett left, Fred gave Emma a concerned

glance. "Should we postpone our meeting? I've had no time to prepare. I doubt you have either."

"It's important, so let's do it," Emma said. "I'm sure the other priests are ready."

Fred and Emma arrived at the meeting, and the five priests were more than ready. Their ideas spewed forth all at once.

Emma held up her hand. "I appreciate your enthusiasm. Hold on to that. First, I want to share my vision for our satellite location at the capital."

"That's a capital idea." Fred smirked. "No pun intended."

The priests gave a polite chuckle while Emma rolled her eyes and shook her head. "I think it makes the most sense for the service to be a feed of what we do here at the new sanctuary. Our focus there should be interacting with people before and especially after the service."

Emma scanned the priests to gauge their reaction. "I hope you'll form a community with the people there. Then we can add programs to meet their needs and help them grow in their faith. Also, I pray we'll positively influence the politicians and their staff."

"I think influence is the whole reason to have a

location in the capital," Fred said. "At least that's why I'm interested."

"I know you have a lot of ideas," Emma told the group. "I'd like to hear them all . . . just not at the same time."

The priests did their best to take turns and not talk over each other, but sometimes their enthusiasm burst forth anyway. Though Emma wanted to focus discussions on the capital, the idea of also holding services in Lakeview County—where the prisoners had been held—continued to pepper their conversation.

In the end, they decided that Fred and two of the priests would pursue opportunities for a satellite location in the capital.

The other two priests would explore possibilities in Lakeview County. "As you meet," Emma said, "please invite Michael and Jerry to provide input. Michael because he's interested in prison reform and Jerry because he's from that area."

The priests agreed, and Emma stood to leave.

"Before we adjourn," Fred said, "I'd like to address a couple of related items. First is a second Senate bill. This one would shut down the Priest Academy until we can get accreditation. That could take years."

"Why do we need accreditation?" Emma asked. "We're just training them so they can do their jobs better. It's not like we're giving them a degree."

"You're correct," Fred said. "That's why I recommend you and I go to the capital to address the senators about this bill, as well as the first one that attacks your role as High Priestess. Perhaps you can even address the full Senate."

Though the idea concerned Emma, she grinned. "I've had visions of me speaking before the Senate. It seems the Sovereign has been preparing me to do this."

"The other item," Fred said, "is to meet with the nation's prison officials to share our plan of using the Lakeview County facility for a new initiative. I propose that Emma and I leave on Monday and attempt to address both on the same day."

Emma gasped. "I'd miss school! And what about all my work here?" But she relaxed as she thought more about it. "Monday sounds good."

Fred wrapped up the meeting. "Remember that these are preliminary discussions about opening satellite locations," he told the group. Then he looked directly at Emma. "Not a word to the media until we have something firm to announce."

14

SITTING WITH THE SOVEREIGN

Emma picked up Montgomery from Ashley's. Though being around people normally energized the High Priestess, at this moment, Emma felt anything but energized. Drained with nothing left. Empty. Mentally, emotionally, and spiritually empty. She shuffled to the cafeteria.

She selected food she could take with her and left the cafeteria without talking to a single person. Emma desperately needed to be alone. She went straight to her room, tossed her supper on the desk, and fed Montgomery. Though she relished her time with Chloe, Emma rejoiced that her roommate would be gone for the weekend.

Montgomery gobbled his food, lapped some water, and plopped on his haunches, looking up at Emma. They both knew what was next. A walk. Emma so didn't want to go out again. She wanted to lie down on her bed and cry herself to sleep. *Is that a sign of weakness? Or is it an acceptable way to release tension?* She wasn't sure.

What she knew was that tears would have to wait. Montgomery came first. She clipped on his leash and the duo headed out. As he pranced at her side, she trudged forward, striving to corral the roiling emotions that surged within her.

They rounded the new auditorium and headed toward the Temple. They took the same path every night. Montgomery knew it well. Up ahead stood Gabe, arms folded, as if waiting for them. He was. No doubt about it.

Her impulse was to snap at him for interrupting her solitude. She didn't want to talk with her mentor. Not tonight. She wanted to wallow in despair. Yet she couldn't take out her frustration on him. He always had her best interest in mind. She liked that about him. Yet his timing was terrible.

"When have you last allocated time to spend in supernatural communication with the Sovereign?" Gabe asked.

Emma gave him an are-you-crazy glare. "I read and study the Holy Text every night."

"But when have you last spent time with the Sovereign?" Gabe punctuated his query with added emphasis.

"I pray every morning when I wake up and every night before I go to sleep. I pray throughout my day, asking for help and thanking the Sovereign for my blessings."

"Yes, but when have you last spent time with the Sovereign?"

"The Sovereign sometimes speaks to me during the day. Every day, I suppose."

"You have now thrice evaded my inquiry. Do not permit your error to repeat." Gabe paused and peered into her eyes. "When have you last spent time with the Sovereign?"

"You mean, when have I last sat in the Sovereign's presence?"

"Precisely."

"It's been a while." Emma hung her head. "I can't remember." She checked her visage in the spiritual realm. Her normal bright white aura had faded. It barely emitted any light at all. She worried it might wither away.

"Your supernatural showdown with the Prime

Minister left you spiritually victorious but drained. After that, you moved forward in your own strength and made no effort to recharge yourself spiritually."

"I messed up. Again. When will I ever learn?"

"You hold expectations that are too lofty," Gabe said. "Remember that you are not yet sixteen years of age. You're a child doing the work of an adult, and in a most arduous role at that."

Emma had never liked Gabe referring to her as a child. It still grated on her. Yet she said nothing.

"Your supernaturally ordained function here at the Temple is of paramount importance," Gabe said. "You're achieving a most admirable outcome in the administration of your assignment. You rightly read and study the Holy Text, far more than most others. In addition, you pray throughout your day and hear the Sovereign speak. All these things are most admirable. Yet they matter little if you don't first attend to your spiritual fitness."

"Does that mean sitting in the Sovereign's presence?"

"Indeed, it does. Nothing matters more. You must attend to it immediately before you—as your generation says—have a total meltdown."

He was right, of course. Gabe was always right. Emma glanced at Montgomery.

Her mentor answered the question she was thinking. "As soon as your young charge accomplishes his requisite business, I suggest you return to your quarters posthaste to bask in the Sovereign's presence."

Emma's eyelids fluttered. "Thank you."

"I must now take my leave of you. I hold immense anticipation of spending the weekend with my reunited family. Among other important activities, we have allocated time to explore the acquisition of a larger abode."

As Gabe walked away, Montgomery looked up at Emma and cocked his head. He squatted and did what he was supposed to do. *Was that supernatural intervention? Thank you, Sovereign.*

Minutes later, they returned to Emma's room. She glanced at her supper and decided it could wait. Turning off the light, she lay on her bed. Montgomery jumped up next to her and snuggled into her embrace. "Mommy's going to go away for a bit—at least my spirit will. You be a good little puppy while I'm gone."

Emma closed her eyes. She extended her free arm—the one not holding Montgomery. "Sovereign Lord, receive my spirit. Open your heavenly home to me."

Emma's spirit left her body and ascended. Montgomery didn't move. He seemed unaware of her departure. Up and up she rose. Her room disappeared from view, then the entire building, and at last the Temple grounds. The world gradually became a distant dot below her. The Sovereign's bright light shone above. Emma's essence rushed forward in glee. *Thank you for receiving me,* Emma thought in her spirit. *Please forgive me for not spending time with you.*

You're already forgiven, came the Sovereign's gentle assurance. *Even before you faltered, I had exonerated you. It's a given.*

The Sovereign embraced Emma. She could stay in this moment forever.

I'm delighted to have you join me in my home once again, came the Sovereign's ethereal words. *But know that you can't come here whenever you wish. Your mission is on earth. You can likewise sit in my presence while remaining in the physical realm. It's just that it takes longer for my children to recharge when they're not here. But if you spent all your time with me in heaven, you'd be no good to me on earth. You'd fail to complete what I called you to do.*

Though deflated, Emma understood. *Got it.* She accepted the Sovereign's explanation. Joy filled

Emma's spirit, as if to burst. She received all the Sovereign gave her. As her spirit recharged, her aura grew brighter.

I want you to visit Barney in prison, came the Sovereign's supernatural words.

What if I don't want to? Emma asked.

Not all that I ask you to do is easy, the Sovereign answered. *Just know that I will be with you and will protect you. He's a hurting man and you can help.*

When? Emma asked.

Soon, came her Lord's reply.

Emma groaned in her spirit. Though it felt like an instant in heaven, Emma wondered how much time had passed on earth. She still struggled to comprehend the truth that the Sovereign lived outside of creation's time-space constraints.

Though Emma didn't have a body in the spiritual realm, she sometimes felt sensations as if she did. Her cheek became damp—wet and cool. The sensation spread as if she was getting a facial massage, not that she had ever gotten one. Her time in the spiritual realm—even though time didn't exist here—was ending.

Emma's spirit withdrew from the Sovereign. The parting was sorrowful, yet the joy she had received from the Almighty would sustain her. Her spirit began the downward trek to earth. Faster and faster she moved. The descent exhilarated her. Her spirit clicked back into her body.

She opened her eyes, and there was Montgomery. He was licking her face.

15

AN UNEXPECTED VISITOR

E mma woke Saturday morning full of energy. She hadn't felt this focused for days, and certainly not since she'd fought the Prime Minister in the spiritual realm. She thanked the Sovereign for restoring her.

Pray for the Prime Minister, came the words of the Divine Spirit into Emma's head.

Emma protested. *I don't want to.*

My children honor me when they pray for their enemies and those who persecute them.

Emma had memorized this passage from the Holy Text. It came from Wisdom 29.3.

She sighed and attempted to focus on the Prime Minister, who was both her enemy and was persecuting her. It took several minutes, but at last she felt ready. "Sovereign Lord, please give me your perspective on the Prime Minister. May she use her time of recovery to turn her thoughts to you. Delay her healing until she's ready to embrace you and work to promote you instead of opposing you. Amen."

Having been obedient to the Divine Spirit's instruction, Emma rushed to embrace the new day.

As she walked to her office after breakfast, a grinning Hernandez joined her. "Good news," he said. "The police have just hauled away all the protesters. It was a brilliant move."

"All of them?" Emma asked. "Everyone?"

"The accuracy of your information thrilled the police. But they couldn't determine a sure way to apprehend all the men and not risk some of them escaping. So they merely waited for the buses to arrive this morning. Before the protesters could exit, officers boarded each bus and redirected them to the police station. That will give them a controlled environment to pull out those wanted for various crimes or questioning."

"What about the rest of them?" Emma asked. "As far as I know, they've done nothing wrong."

"They'll be held for twenty-four hours and then released—assuming there's nothing to charge them with. At minimum, that will disrupt their protest for a day. But I suspect it will lose steam, and they'll disperse. The protest may be over."

"Thanks for your part in making it happen," Emma told Hernandez.

"It's all because of your information," he said.

"All credit goes to the Sovereign."

Hernandez left Emma, and she soon arrived at her office. Scarlett awaited her. "I did what you said and followed the money! It came from G. S. Acerman."

"The name sounds familiar," Emma said. "But why?"

"He's a high-tech mogul who uses his wealth to promote liberal causes. He reportedly funneled millions into the Prime Minister's election through back-door channels. And now, he's funding the protesters."

"Though I don't like it, he has every right to donate his money to whoever he wants."

"You're correct, but if he and the Prime Minister colluded on the protests, that's illegal and they both face arrest."

"Colluded?"

"It means they acted in secret to launch an organized protest against you. It's surely no coincidence that the protests started just after the Prime Minister threatened you. All I need to do is find proof."

Lane bounced through the doorway. "Morning, ladies. I figured out what Barney and the Prime Minister were doing with the email account."

Emma and Scarlett looked at Lane, their eyes begging him to continue.

"Whenever anyone sends an email," Lane explained, "that message is stored on each server it passes through as it travels to its destination. Once sent, it's impossible to keep an email private. Yet a workaround is to leave the message in draft mode and never send it. I think Barney and the Prime Minister were both logging into this account to leave messages for each other. If we read the draft message as a back-and-forth conversation made over time, it suddenly makes sense. I think we have a day's worth of communication."

"If only we could go back further," Scarlett lamented.

Lane nodded.

Emma perked up. "When we looked into the security camera footage of Barney's visitors, it only stored content for twenty-four hours before deleting it. But Barney had paid for a deluxe plan. A feature he wasn't aware of is that it uploaded the files to permanent storage before they were erased. I wonder if he might have paid for a deluxe email package that did the same thing?"

"Great idea!" Lane walked around the desk and sat in front of the computer. He stretched his hands over the keyboard and wiggled his fingers. "If you ladies give me some space, I'll check into it. Since we cancelled today's driver's training for the wedding, I've got all morning."

Emma and Scarlett left the office and eased the door shut behind them. Once outside, Emma turned to the reporter. "Maybe the Prime Minister and G. S. Acerman communicated in the same way."

"That's an interesting idea," Scarlett said. "Let's see what Lane finds out and go from there."

As the two of them continued talking, Montgomery plopped onto the floor. His head pivoted from one to the other as they spoke. It was as if he were following their discussion.

Approaching footsteps halted their conversation. They turned around. Ashley strode toward them.

"What's wrong?" Emma asked. "Is it something about the wedding?"

Ashley shook her head. "Didn't you get my text?"

Emma reached for her back pocket. She gasped. "Must've left my phone in my room. At least I hope I did."

"I rescheduled Montgomery's training session for this morning," Ashley said. "I texted you and have been looking for you for the past fifteen minutes." She checked the time. "If we leave right now, we can still make it."

"You're getting married in a few hours. Montgomery's training doesn't matter."

"If I don't distract myself," Ashley said, "I'll go crazy with worry about all the things that could go wrong."

"Nothing is going to go wrong," Emma said. Then she questioned her confident statement. She prayed silently. *May Ashley and Topher's wedding ceremony come off without a hitch.*

"It's all good," she told Ashley. "Nothing to worry about."

16

MARRIED AT LAST

Emma and Ashley spent the next several hours hanging out. Emma tried to distract Ashley and keep her from worrying about the wedding. At last, it was time.

Emma led Ashley to the first dressing room behind the sanctuary stage to put on her wedding robe. The second dressing room was for Topher, but he wasn't there. Emma went to her dressing room to put on her regular Sunday robe.

Seconds later, a robed Ashley knocked on the frame of the open door of Emma's dressing room. Ashley lugged her huge cosmetics case at her side.

Emma smiled. "I know you powder my forehead and nose every Sunday, but today is your day. No one's going to be looking at me."

"I want you to look your best too. Topher only objected a little when I checked on him. Now it's your turn."

Emma closed her eyes and Ashley went to work. As usual, it only took seconds. When Emma opened her eyes, a grinning Topher stood in the doorway.

"Since you're both here," Emma said, "I'd like to pray before the ceremony."

She reached out and held Ashley's hand and extended her other one to Topher. He approached and clasped it. Then the couple joined hands to complete the circle.

"Lord, we give this ceremony to you," Emma prayed. "May all we do here honor you and bring glory to your name. Bless Ashley and Topher in their marriage. May they put you first in all that they do. May they serve as an example to encourage others, both those who are now married and those not-yet-married couples who will witness today's ceremony. So be it."

"Amen," Ashley said.

Then Topher echoed her with an "Amen" of his own.

"Any last-minute questions?" Emma asked.

They both shook their heads.

"Go sit with your families. We'll begin shortly."

After they left, Emma breathed out slowly and inhaled with deliberation. As her lungs filled, she envisioned an extra anointing of the Divine Spirit filling her. With supernatural confidence, she left her dressing room and moved to the stage. She sat on the small chair next to the cathedra like she did for each Sunday service.

Mindful of her prayers for not-yet-married couples, Emma scanned the crowd. In the front row to her far left sat Topher's dad—Christopher—and Angie. Their wedding would take place next Saturday. Jennifer and David also sat toward the front. They'd likely be married in a few months. Chloe sat with Lane. They held hands. Though they were moving toward marriage, just like she and Joshua, that would be at least a couple of years away.

Speaking of Joshua, her eyes quickly found him. He sat with his family. In the same row was Emma's family. Emma's brother, Brayden, sat next to Joshua's sister, Sarah. Emma knew her brother had a crush on Sarah but wondered what she thought about him. They both squirmed.

Scarlett sat in the back, poised to take notes for her coverage of the ceremony. Emma didn't know the stunning guy sitting next to her, but they certainly looked like a couple—a smart one at that.

Ezra sat in the front row, strumming a zither. It was a historically accurate replica. He'd also use it in tomorrow's first service in the ancient Temple. Surprisingly, Aurora sat next to him. Surely it wasn't coincidence. They had been spending a lot of time together as work on the welcome center progressed. Was Emma witnessing a budding romance?

Having given everyone a moment to focus on what was about to occur, Emma stood and approached the center of the stage, where the dais normally stood. Ezra stopped playing.

"We're here today to witness the holy union of Topher Perkins and Ashley Smythe," Emma proclaimed. "We'll pattern today's ceremony after what we read in the Holy Text. From now on, we'll follow this for all wedding ceremonies." Then Emma read the passage that described the marriage ceremony between Mateo and Yael.

Emma glanced at Ashley on her right. The young woman dipped her head. Emma turned to her left. Topher nodded. They were ready.

Emma stretched out her arms to each side. "May the intended and their families rise." Ashley and her parents stood on one side of the auditorium, while Topher, his dad, and Angie stood on the other.

Emma turned to face Topher. "What is your intent?"

"To be forever joined with my beloved Ashley," Topher answered.

"Does your family support you in this?" Emma asked.

Christopher and Angie responded. "We do."

Emma pivoted to face Ashley. "What is your intent?"

"To be forever joined with my beloved Topher," Ashley responded.

"Does your family support you in this?" Emma asked.

Ashley's parents responded. "We do."

"As you approach me to officiate your wedding," Emma said, "know that you are also approaching the Sovereign. This is a holy union intended to last for the rest of your lives. Do you understand the solemn pledge you are about to make?"

"We do," came Topher and Ashley's confirmation.

Emma nodded to Ezra. He resumed playing,

and she gestured for the couple and their parents to approach.

Ezra played a rhythmic melody, with the parties taking one step closer on each measure. At the base of the stage, their parents turned and sat in the front row, while Topher and Ashley ascended the steps on each side of the platform. They stopped when they reached Emma in the middle, facing one another. Ezra stopped playing.

"Topher," Emma said, "what is your pledge to Ashley?"

"To spend the rest of my life with her and strive to love her every day the way the Sovereign loves me."

"Ashley," Emma said, "what is your pledge to Topher?"

"To spend the rest of my life with him and strive to love him every day the way the Sovereign loves me."

"What do you have to symbolize your pledge?" Emma asked.

They each held up a short rope. Emma took the end of each one and tied them together in a knot. She pulled it tight. Then the couple tested it. The knot held firm.

"Based on your lifelong pledge to each other

before your family, friends, and the Sovereign, I declare you to be spiritually and legally married. May the Lord bless your union and your future children."

Topher and Ashley took their last step toward each other and embraced. Their family and friends stood and applauded.

Emma reveled in what had just happened. It was a holy moment, and she had successfully performed her first wedding. *Thank you, Sovereign.* One down and two to go.

17

SUNDAY SURPRISE

Emma left her room on Sunday morning to start her day. She had a jam-packed one. Today they would add a fourth service—the one at the ancient Temple. Emma felt she should make all four—at least part of each one.

After breakfast, she'd scoot to the ancient Temple for its inaugural service. Then the new auditorium for its first service, dash to the old auditorium for their service, and then return to the new auditorium for its second service. She'd give the message at both services in the new auditorium. After lunch with her family, she and Fred would fly to the capital for their meetings on Monday. Yes, she would have a jam-packed day.

Fred awaited her outside the priests' quarters. Grinning, he sat in a golf cart. "Surprise!"

Emma shook her head. "What's this?"

"It's a golf cart, of course."

"Yes, but why do you have one? You don't golf, and there's no course nearby."

"It arrived yesterday. It's for you."

"I don't golf either." Emma scowled. "I don't want to and don't have the time." Then she grew sober. "Seems the last High Priest was always golfing. Is that part of the job? Must I play too?"

Fred threw his head back and let out a belly laugh. The cart shook as he bellowed. "A golf cart isn't only for golf. I got it to help you move between services. But this is not a toy, and it's just for your use on Sunday mornings."

"Got it. But I don't have my driver's license yet."

Fred chuckled. "You don't need a license to drive a golf cart. If you can drive a car, you can certainly manage this."

"I'm not doing so well at driving a car. Topher says I need extra practice."

The pleased smirk on Fred's face vanished. "I wasn't aware of that. Nevertheless, it's much easier than driving a car. You go forward, you steer, and you brake. The one rule is to not hit anyone or anything. And always go slow." Fred slid over and patted the seat. "Let's practice."

As Emma drove the short path from the priests' quarters to the cafeteria, she confirmed that driving a golf cart was indeed much easier than a car. For extra practice, she circled the cafeteria, making two laps before stopping outside.

"Well done," Fred proclaimed. "I declare you ready to drive a golf cart."

After eating breakfast with the priests, Emma returned to her new ride. She jumped in with a grin and drove straight to the ancient Temple. If not for the cart, she'd have had to run the entire distance—another thing she didn't excel at. She parked in back and entered the side door. She slipped into the old gray robe she had worn at her first service as High Priestess. Though she still didn't like it, she appreciated that it best aligned with an ancient Temple service.

Ezra played the prelude using his zither. With the place packed, people stood in the back. A few even peered in from the outside. One attendee caught Emma's notice. It was Aurora. She sat next to Ezra in the front row.

Emma opened the service with a greeting and a

prayer. "We'll be conducting our services here as closely as possible to what we read in the Holy Text. We want to embrace our heritage and use it to better inform our worship of the Sovereign. This is our first service here, so please be patient as we fine-tune it in the weeks ahead."

Ezra stood to lead the rest of the service. Emma was to observe—and worship. Yet there was no place for her to sit. The only open spot was next to Aurora, where Ezra had just vacated. Emma joined the affable architect.

Ezra and the other priests did a great job with the service. Emma appreciated seeing many aspects she had read about in the Holy Text. The rhythms of the rituals filled her with awe, and she felt the Sovereign's pleasure.

As the service wound down, Ezra called Emma forward to give the parting blessing. This wasn't part of the plan, but Emma was ready. "Thank you for experiencing the service here with us today," she told those gathered. "Please join us again next Sunday." She raised her arms. "May the Sovereign bless you in the week ahead and guide your paths. May you go forth with peace and joy. Amen." Then she lowered her arms and grinned. "See you next week." She waved goodbye.

Ezra strummed the zither as the people exited, while Emma scooted to the back. She removed her robe, exited the building, and hopped on her golf cart. She was off to the new auditorium.

Emma parked by the back entrance and headed straight to her dressing room. Emma pulled on her pink robe, and Ashley swept in to powder her forehead. The young bride glowed.

"Not that I'm not happy to see you," Emma said, "but we gave you the day off. My forehead can survive one Sunday without your attention."

Ashley gave a dismissive wave with her hand. "Nonsense. I'm here to serve you and the Sovereign."

"What's Topher think about you being here today?" Emma asked.

"She has my full support." The grinning groom stood in the doorway. He beamed almost as much as his bride. "It's just that I can't bear to let her out of my sight."

Emma blessed them both and hustled to the stage. She welcomed the people to the service. As Mark stood to lead the next part, Emma eased off the platform. Back in her dressing room, Emma removed her pink robe and made a hasty departure.

The trek to the old auditorium was longer than

her first two journeys. Once there, she donned her light blue robe and gave the welcoming greeting. As Gavin rose to lead the rest of the service, Emma edged away. Then she removed her blue robe, drove back to the new auditorium, and pulled on her pink robe. She eased up to the stage to give the message just as the final worship song wound down.

The pace of her morning so far left her exhilarated and exhausted. And she had one more service to go. She retreated to her dressing room and sat in the Sovereign's presence until they called her for the second service at the new auditorium, her fourth and final one of the day.

18

EMMA'S FIRST FLIGHT

Later that day, Emma plopped into her seat on the plane. "Boarding went a lot easier than I expected," she said to Fred. "I thought we'd have to wait in line, that it would take hours."

"Normally that's true," Fred said. "But they gave us special treatment because you're the High Priestess."

Emma scrunched up her nose. "I was sure no one would recognize me wearing a ball cap and glasses."

"No one will, but your name is on the ticket. That's also why we got a free upgrade to first class."

"Does that mean the rest of the seats aren't as nice as these?"

Fred nodded. He jabbed his thumb behind him. "Back there, they're packed in like sardines."

"I don't like getting special treatment just because I'm the High Priestess."

"Be thankful when it happens, don't be upset when it doesn't, and most importantly, never expect it."

Emma pondered his wisdom. "In other words, stay humble."

"Precisely."

Emma rummaged through her backpack and pulled out her algebra book.

"Before you dive into Monday's schoolwork, let's talk about tomorrow's schedule," Fred said.

Emma shoved her book aside. "What's there to talk about? I trust you with the schedule, and I trust the Sovereign to tell me what to say."

Fred pressed forward. "At eight we're meeting with Senator Warren, who introduced the bill to remove you as High Priestess. At nine, we'll meet with the sponsors of the other bill that will shut down our school. We have a 10:30 meeting with the Prison Oversight Authority to present our vision for the facility in Lakeview County. Michael's proposal, by the way, is brilliant. At lunch, I'll introduce you to some of my political contacts. Then, at two, you're scheduled to present to the entire Senate. That rarely happens, and I want you to make the most of the opportunity. We must discuss what you will say."

"I got overwhelmed when you tried to prepare me to meet with the Prime Minister, and that didn't go well," Emma said. "When we meet with the Senate, I'm going to rely on the Sovereign to guide my words."

"From a human standpoint, that's an ill-advised strategy," Fred countered. "Yet from a spiritual perspective, relying on divine insight may be the best way to go. It certainly seems to work for you. Even so, I remain apprehensive."

"I have faith."

Fred was quiet, likely thinking about Emma's presentation before the Senate. He sighed but then perked up. "Ezra reported that the inaugural service in the ancient Temple was a success."

"I really liked it," Emma said. "I think most everyone felt that way."

"Ezra said it was standing room only," Fred said. "He recommends next week we add a second Temple service at 9:00."

"I was thinking the same thing. I can make that work."

Fred shook his head. "It was too tight for you today, trying to take part in four services. I can't imagine five."

Emma had a ready answer. "It was foolish of me to open the first service in the new sanctuary, leave to give the greeting in the old one, and then return to give the message in the new. That's when things almost fell apart. I won't make that mistake again."

"You do seem to learn from your mistakes," Fred said.

"That's how I roll," Emma confirmed. "The Holy Text says, 'Learn from the past to inform today and usher in a better tomorrow.' It's from the book of Prophecy, but I don't remember where."

"Nor do I."

"Next week I'm supposed to give the message in the old sanctuary," Emma said. "I can open the first service in the new sanctuary, give my message in the old one, and make it back to the new to close the second service. That's doable. Plus, there are no conflicts for the two Temple services. My new golf cart will make it a breeze. Easy peasy."

"I'm concerned that you feel the need to be at

every service," Fred said. "I wonder if it may be ego or pride that's driving you to do that."

Emma smiled as she shook her head. "It's the Sovereign."

"Once again," Fred said, "your supernatural perspective surpasses my own." He squirmed. "Perhaps you have some insight about our attendance today. Despite an extra two hundred people at the Temple, we were down about ten percent overall."

"I don't care about numbers," Emma said. "Quality over quantity."

"I knew you'd say that, but there's more," Fred said. "Ever since that Sunday protest, Hernandez has stationed a guard to observe people as they enter the Temple grounds. That way, the guards can quickly spot a potential problem and react. This morning, the guard reported many cars that slowed down to turn into our entrance, veered off at the last moment, and sped away. Others drove up the drive, made a U-turn, and left. Any thoughts on that?"

Emma hung her head. "I'm afraid it's my fault," she mumbled.

"How can that be your fault?"

"After my supernatural confrontation with the

Prime Minister, I declared that no evil may enter our campus. I didn't mean to include people. Only spirits. I suspect we all have a bit of evil in us, yet through the Sovereign we overcome it. Others may search for truth, even though evil still lurks in them. I wonder if they were the people who left?"

"Your conclusion seems reasonable," Fred said. "Can you fix it?"

"I don't see why not."

"Now explain what you meant about the supernatural confrontation with the Prime Minister."

"Last Thursday, the Prime Minister's spirit attacked me while I was sleeping. She caught me off guard and almost killed me, but just before she did, Chloe distracted her. Then Chloe woke Joshua. The three of us fought and defeated the Prime Minister in the spiritual realm."

Fred stroked his beard. "Thursday night? Early Friday morning, the Prime Minister was rushed to the hospital. The details remain vague. Any connection?"

"I'm afraid that's my fault too," Emma said. "Though the three of us attacked her spirit, I took the lead. We quickly defeated her. What happens in the spiritual realm can affect our bodies."

Fred gave a slow nod. "So she ended up in the hospital and you three were unscathed?"

Emma shook her head. "Chloe and I also had physical injuries. The Sovereign healed us. But I prayed that the Prime Minister wouldn't receive healing until she turned to the Sovereign. Was I wrong to do that?"

19

MONDAY MORNING MEETINGS

Emma fidgeted as she waited with Fred in Senator Warren's reception area on Monday morning. "Politics is equal parts patience and preparedness to strike at the right moment," Fred whispered to Emma.

For the first time in about forever, she wore a dress—a knee-length navy blue beauty with subtle white polka dots. It boasted a trim fit, both modest and professional—at least for a 15-year-old.

"I don't think I've ever seen you in a dress," Fred said. "It's most appropriate for today and looks nice. It also makes you look older."

Emma squirmed. "Ah . . . thank you. I guess."

After twenty more minutes of mostly patient

waiting, a young man stepped out from the inner office. Emma liked him right away. His spirit had a light red countenance. "Senator Warren asked me to express his regret that he will not be able to meet with you today. My name is Xavier. If you'll tell me why you're here, I'll relay your message to the Senator."

Xavier gestured to the open door behind him. Emma and Fred walked in. To the right was a luxurious meeting space, complete with a rich mahogany table and lush leather chairs. After exchanging greetings and shaking hands, the three of them sat.

"Let me begin by thanking you for the opportunity to talk with you this morning," Fred said, "We'd like to share with you our perspective on—"

"We don't want to waste your time," Emma interrupted, "and wish to ask the Senator to withdraw his bill prohibiting me from being High Priestess.

Xavier's professional smile morphed into a genuine one. "I appreciate your candor, High Priestess."

"Please call me Emma."

"I appreciate your candor, Emma. Off the

record, Senator Warren didn't want to introduce the bill, but the Prime Minister called in a favor he couldn't refuse. Also off the record, public response to the bill coming into the Senator's office is fifty to one against it. It's most unpopular."

Emma smiled. "Please add two more people to the list of those opposed to it." She stood. "Thank you for listening. Have a great day." Emma gestured goodbye and turned to leave. Then she stopped and spun around when the Sovereign revealed a bit of supernatural insight to her. "You're wondering what to get your mother for her birthday. She'd really like a silk scarf with a blue floral print."

Xavier smiled. "That would be perfect! And I'll be sure to let the Senator know your concerns."

A bewildered Fred followed Emma out of Senator Warren's office. Without a word, he led her down the hall, up two flights of stairs, and around the corner into a conference room. It was half full of people.

Emma worked her way around the table, introducing herself, shaking hands, and thanking each one for coming. Most of them were aides waiting for their senators to arrive. But only three senators were there at 9:00.

At the Sovereign's direction, Emma walked to the podium and cleared her throat. "I know you all have busy schedules, and I don't want to take any more of your time than necessary."

"The lead higher education lobbyist had wanted to be here today," one senator stated, "but her flight encountered delays and won't arrive until this evening. She has significant concerns about your intent and your process." He looked the oldest of the three senators and the sourest. "That's why they're insisting you go through the accreditation process before proceeding."

"Our Priest Academy is to teach ministry staff what they need to know to do their jobs," Emma said. "It's job-related training and not a degree alternative. We have nothing against seminary programs. We support them and what they do. It's just that we provide specific training about the Holy Text. If any seminaries want to do that, too, we're happy to share our materials with them."

"That is helpful information to know," the senator said. "Will you issue a statement to that effect?"

Emma saw Fred nodding from the back of the room and answered for him. "Certainly. We'll send you copies before we post it." She scanned the room and sensed there was nothing more to add. "I thank everyone for being here, especially the senators. I trust all aides will pass on this information to their bosses. Everyone have a great day." Emma winked, waved, and whooshed from the room. It was a five-minute meeting.

As the driver took them to the Prison Oversight Authority, Fred at last broke the tension. "That's not at all how I would have handled either meeting, and you completely went against protocol." He groaned. "Yet I sense you said exactly what needed to be said and accomplished what we needed to do. Despite my misgivings, the Sovereign led you well."

"I had planned to watch you," Emma said. "But the Sovereign had other ideas. Sorry."

"Don't apologize for obeying the Sovereign. Do you plan to lead our next meeting as well?"

Emma shook her head. "Hope not. I haven't even read Michael's proposal."

Fred stood before the Prison Oversight Authority as Emma passed out their information packet. After thanking them for their presence, Fred shared their vision for the prison facility in Lakeview County and went through the proposal in painstaking detail. To conclude his 30-minute presentation, he asked for questions.

The director leaned back and crossed his arms. "What does the High Priestess have to say?"

Shocked, Emma rose slowly, praying for supernatural insight. As she opened her mouth to speak, the Sovereign implanted words into her mind. "During my time as High Priestess, my focus has been on reform. We've seen an increase in attendance, record donations, and deeper engagement. Most importantly, people have grown in their faith, while the priests and staff have renewed enthusiasm for their work."

"While most impressive," the man said, "this is a prison and not a ministry."

"So true," Emma replied. "If you want to maintain the status quo, then turn down our proposal. But if you're open to a fresh approach, what do you have to lose by giving us a shot? Your budget will stay the same, and we'll cover any extra costs. We'll take care of everything. If we fail, then decommission the facility as planned. But if we succeed—and I'm sure we will—the impact will be huge."

Emma smiled as she scanned the room. "I'm committed to making our world a better place. Will you join me?"

The room was quiet for a moment as the director's head bobbed, slowly at first and then with more intention. He smiled. "Let's make it happen."

20

EMMA'S VISION

At lunch, Emma met Fred's political contacts. They were all relationships he had formed during his undergrad studies in political science. Being around them, Emma sensed a spark igniting in his soul. He was meant to be here, to serve the Sovereign in the political sphere. Knowing this, Emma was at last ready to release him to the capital.

Another thing they learned at lunch—off the record, of course—was that the Prime Minister was gravely ill. Many speculated she'd never leave the hospital. Emma questioned even more seriously her prayer that the Prime Minister would not receive healing until she turned to the Sovereign.

Should I have not prayed that?

That concern stayed with Emma, even as she rose to address the Senate later that afternoon. Every senator was there. A mass of people packed the observation area. The media was also present, but cameras and phones were banned from today's meeting.

As she slowly scanned the attentive crowd, Emma breathed a prayer to be filled with peace and to speak what the Sovereign told her to say. She smiled as she waited for divine insight. After a dramatic pause, it came in a mighty whoosh.

"Today I want to share with you something I recently found out about our political system. I didn't learn this in school. I don't think anyone did. The position of Prime Minister, the Senate, and the judiciary were all established a few hundred years ago to extend the High Priest's authority. The idea was to lessen his workload. But over time, a political system emerged that opposed the religion that birthed it. And I was surprised to learn that both the Prime Minister and the High Priest have veto power over any Senate bill."

The crowd's reaction to her statement suggested that most people didn't know this either.

"I'm here today to ask for a recommitment to the vision that birthed our political system. From now on, I pledge to work closely with the Prime Minister to accomplish that. Later today, I hope to visit her in the hospital and pray for her recovery."

Some Senators smiled and others gasped.

"I leave you with this parting blessing." Emma raised her arms just like she did at the Sunday services. "May the Sovereign bless you and all your work. May our Lord guide your discussions, direct your decisions, and receive honor through all that you do. Receive supernatural joy and peace as you move forward."

Emma lowered her arms and took a step back from the podium.

Some senators and most of the visitors rose as one and applauded. Soon everyone was standing. Emma smiled, signaled goodbye, and sauntered from the Senate floor.

Emma and Fred exited the Senate building to a cacophony of reporters armed with cameras and wielding microphones. She had had visions of this, except that her visions included flashbulbs going off. That was so old school. But just then, a reporter's phone emitted a flash of light. Everyone glared at him.

"Sorry," he mumbled. "I must have messed up

the settings." He frowned at his phone as he punched buttons.

Several security officers held the reporters back. Everyone shouted their questions at once.

One reporter's voice rose above all others. "What did you tell the Senate?"

"I reminded them of the historic connection between our politics and our faith," Emma answered. "It's important we embrace this from now on."

Another reporter got her attention. "I understand you ended your time before the Senate with a blessing, just like at a Sunday service." He smirked. "Did you forget where you were?"

"Not at all. A blessing is appropriate to anyone in any situation," Emma said. "We're wrong if we try to separate our faith from the rest of our lives."

"Do you really intend to visit the Prime Minister in the hospital?" screamed a third reporter. "You earlier claimed she threatened you."

"She did indeed threaten me, but Scripture says we're to pray for our enemies. I've been praying for her ever since she entered the hospital. That has softened my heart toward her. My next step is to pray for her healing."

As reporters shouted more questions, Emma

and Fred's car pulled up to the curb in front of the Senate building. Fred stepped forward and held up his hands. "That's all we have time for today."

"Does that mean you'll have something more for us tomorrow?" asked another reporter as Emma and Fred brushed by.

"Be at the hospital tomorrow morning," Emma said. "I foresee that the Prime Minister will be released then."

Emma ducked into the car and slid over to make room for Fred. As the car eased away, reporters trailed alongside, peppering her with more questions.

She just waved.

"Please take us to the hospital," Emma told the driver.

He gave her a questioning look in his rearview mirror but then nodded. "As you wish."

"We'll never get past security," Fred said.

"We must try," Emma responded. "Whether or not I talk with the Prime Minister, I will pray for her healing."

21

GETTING PAST SECURITY

Emma and Fred did indeed get past the first level of security stationed at the elevator doors. Yet the officer positioned in the Prime Minister's hallway shook his head as they neared him. He held up his hand to signal them to halt. Then he planted his feet and shook his head again.

Emma and Fred stopped. "You stay here and video me," Emma whispered to Fred. "I'm going in."

She sauntered up to the guard. He stiffened as she approached. When she relaxed her shoulders, so did he. "I'm here on an urgent mission on behalf of the Sovereign to heal the Prime Minister. May I pass?"

He didn't say a word or even blink. When she eased past him, he didn't stop her. Soon she was at the door of the Prime Minister's hospital room.

But that guard wouldn't budge. "I'm not unsympathetic to what you want to accomplish, High Priestess." She gave a slight bow and dropped her voice to a mere whisper. "The Prime Minister is in a coma and not expected to make it through the night. Sorry, but you're too late."

Emma thanked the guard and turned away. Facing Fred, who stood down the hall recording her, she pulled out her phone to also video herself. "I'm here at the hospital to visit the Prime Minister," she whispered. "Though I'm not allowed to see her, I will pray for her." Emma placed her free hand on the wall outside of the Prime Minister's hospital room. "In the name of the Sovereign, I declare complete healing on the Prime Minister. Restore her to full health. May she be released tomorrow. Amen."

Emma stopped recording, returned to Fred, and posted her video online.

Fred had also stopped his recording. "I guess you won't be needing this." His finger hovered over the delete button.

Emma shook her head. "Send it to Scarlett. She may need it tomorrow."

Fred did and then checked the time. "If we hurry, we could still make our flight." They dashed to the car and were soon speeding to the airport.

Emma's phone rang. "Must be important. It's a video call from Lane." She pressed the answer button. "I'm with Frederick. What's up?"

"Too much info to cover in a text. Good news! I've accessed the backups of Barney's private email account. There are a ton of entries. Scarlett's been poring over them all day. She says it confirms the Prime Minister was part of the plot to kill the former High Priest and the attempt to kill you. Scarlett plans to pull an all-nighter and go public tomorrow."

He pivoted the phone to Scarlett. Her tired face lit up when she saw Emma. "Not only does this give more evidence to convict Barney, but the Prime Minister will go down with him. He also promised to divert Temple donations to fund her election. There's enough fraud evidence here to put them both behind bars for the rest of their lives."

"Great job," Emma said. "Just don't push yourself too hard."

Before Emma could see Scarlett's reaction, Lane

pivoted the phone back to himself. "In one day's message, Barney told the Prime Minister how to set up a private email account like this one so she could secretly communicate with G. S. Acerman. I found that account but can't log in. Any ideas for the password?"

Emma thought and then prayed for supernatural insight.

It's a phrase based on Barney's name, said the Sovereign to Emma. *You can figure it out.*

Emma waited for more, but that was it. She thought back to her interaction with the Prime Minister, who referred to Barney as Bernard—even though that wasn't his real name. She then recalled an odd phrase the Prime Minister had used.

"You've got something, don't you?" Lane asked.

"Yep! Try 'my beloved Bernard'."

"With or without spaces? What about caps?"

Emma shrugged. "Don't know. Try different combinations."

Lane lay his phone on the desk, giving Emma a clear view of the ceiling. He began typing. "Nope." He resumed keying. "Not that." More clicking. "Not that either," followed by a flurry of keystrokes. "Bingo! I'm in! It's title caps with spaces."

"Anything else?" Emma asked.

Lane didn't respond.

"You still there?"

"Yeah . . . Just a sec . . . Yep, this account has daily backups too. Looks like a ton of info."

"Just don't push yourself too hard, either."

As Emma stared at her phone, the call disconnected.

22

HOMEWARD BOUND

Emma and Fred stood in line at the airport. She shifted to her right. Then to her left. She sucked in a deep breath and closed her eyes. To distract herself from the seemingly endless wait, she shifted her mind to happier thoughts. She soon envisioned her puppy.

Emma sighed. "I sure miss Montgomery. We've never been apart this long."

"Is Ashley watching him?" Fred asked.

"I'm sure she would have if I had asked, but Joshua's sister, Sarah, offered to watch him while I was gone. Maggie—their mom—will drop off Montgomery with Chloe tonight when she picks up Joshua."

When Emma's phone chirped, her eyes lit up.

"Maybe that's an update." But when she glanced at the screen, all the excitement drained from her face. She sighed—again. "It's an unknown number." Emma quickly scanned the message and then read aloud for Fred to hear. "High Priestess or not, if you ever try to contact the Prime Minister again, we will have you arrested. Count on it."

Before Fred could stop her, Emma sent a hasty response. "Don't threaten me! I'll only do what the Sovereign tells me to do!!!"

She fully expected Fred to reprimand her for acting before thinking. But he did not. Instead, they shuffled forward in silence.

At last, Emma broke their quiet. "When you move to the capital, we'll need to fill your slot for the Sunday services. Though Ezra can handle the Temple services, it'll just be Mark and me to cover all three auditorium services."

"We established that for someone to teach at our Sunday services," Fred said, "they'd need to have scored at least ninety on the Holy Text exam. That leaves Gabe and Joshua as our only candidates. Incidentally, since I only got an eighty-three, I shouldn't be speaking at all."

As she considered what Fred had said, Emma stared at the long line in front of them. "Gabe can act a bit odd at times. As far as Joshua, we promised that my disciples wouldn't speak or teach until they were adults. So he's got over two years to wait."

"I propose we move forward with both of them," Fred replied. "We'll take small incremental steps to introduce them to the people. That will give them time to hone their speaking skills and become more comfortable in front of an audience."

Emma worried that neither would be up to the challenge, but prayed she was wrong.

"Let me handle it," Fred said. "I'll run it by your executive team and then get a buy-in from all the priests. I also know Gavin's interested. He scored an eighty-seven on his test, so he's the next closest to being ready."

At last, they reached the security checkpoint. Emma handed the official her ticket. The woman scanned it and then gasped. "You shouldn't be in this line." Then she looked up and scrutinized Emma. "I'm sorry. I assumed you were someone else." She handed the ticket back to Emma. "Please proceed."

Emma smiled, mostly to herself. *I guess my disguise is working.*

After clearing security, they plopped into chairs at the waiting area for their gate. Fred pulled out his laptop to work on the statement of intent about their Priest Academy. He finished it in no time and turned his laptop for Emma to read it.

"It's brilliant," Emma said. "Once they read this, I'm sure they'll withdraw their bill."

"One can only hope," Fred said.

"I prefer to pray first and then hope," Emma retorted.

Fred emailed their statement to the aide who had agreed to disperse it to all the bill's sponsors. "That part's done. I'll make my public announcement tomorrow. Maybe Scarlett will want to be part of it."

23

AIRPORT OPPORTUNITIES

A plane taxied up to their gate. Emma and Fred watched the exiting passengers flood into the terminal.

Fred gave Emma a quick jab with his elbow. "That's the lead rep for the higher education lobby." He pointed at a casually dressed woman who carried herself with dignity. "I'm sure of it. Let's talk to her." Fred rushed off.

When Emma decided to follow him, she had to hurry to catch up. By the time she did, Fred had already introduced himself to the unsuspecting lobbyist. The woman's skeptical eyes relaxed a bit when Emma moved to Fred's side. "I apologize for not being present at your meeting today," the lobbyist said to Fred. "But I lacked the needed notice to arrange for airfare. Certainly you understand."

Fred assured her that he did, summarized their intentions with the Priest Academy, and got her email address so he could send her an advanced copy of tomorrow's statement.

"This is all well and good," the lobbyist said. She scrutinized Fred while ignoring Emma. "But what matters most to me is what the High Priestess thinks."

"I'm fine with it," Emma interjected. "I'm behind it one hundred percent."

The lobbyist diverted her penetrating stare from Fred to glance at Emma. "And who are you?"

"I'm Emma Barlow, the High Priestess."

The woman shook her head. "No you're not."

Emma grinned, removed her glasses, and took off her ball cap. "How about now?"

The woman gasped. "Please forgive my blunder, My Lord," she sputtered and then bowed. Trembling, she started to kneel, but Emma stopped her.

"We're open to work with you," Emma said. "Feel free to schedule a visit. We'll show you what we do and share our materials with any school that wants them."

Still shaking a bit, the woman attempted to regain her composure. "If Frederick's statement aligns with what you just told me, I don't foresee a problem. Assuming that's the case, I'll ask the senators to withdraw their bill." She smiled at Emma for the first time and gave a cute curtsy before she hurried away.

As Emma and Fred returned to their seats by the gate, a woman hesitantly approached Emma, her left shoulder drooping. "Please forgive me for intruding, My Lord, but I saw your video that declared healing on the Prime Minister." The woman stared at the ground. "Will you heal my shoulder? It's been giving me problems for years. The doctors can't fix it, but I have faith you can."

"The Sovereign can. And please call me Emma."

Still staring at her feet, the woman nodded. "Yes, Emma," she whispered.

"Please look at me," Emma said. When the woman didn't, Emma reached out and gently touched her chin. The woman glanced up. Her eyes emoted equal parts pain and hope.

"May I lay my hand on your shoulder?"
"Yes."

Emma reached out, her hand hovering over the

woman's left shoulder. She lowered her fingers and made the slightest contact. "By the Sovereign's power, I declare complete healing of your shoulder."

The woman gulped. Her shoulder popped back to its normal position, and she stood fully erect. "The pain is gone. It feels fine!" She rotated her shoulder as tears streamed down her cheeks. "I'm healed!" As Emma withdrew her hand, the woman grabbed it, brought it to her lips, and kissed it. "Thank you." She gave Emma a slight bow of respect. "Thank you so much."

A young man walked up. The woman moved aside, and he stepped forward. "I have an important meeting tomorrow. Will you bless my presentation?"

Emma brought her right hand to his forehead. "May the Sovereign bless you at your meeting, fill you with peace, and grant you favor."

The man's face lit up. He grabbed her hand and shook it. "Thank you!"

A second man edged up. "I've been suffering from debilitating headaches. Can you heal me?"

"The Sovereign can." Emma moved her hand to the right side of his head and pronounced healing.

"I feel a difference already. Thank you, My Lord."

Though Emma wanted to correct him, a line stood behind him. Some asked for healing and others for a blessing. She responded to each request.

After several minutes, Fred tugged at her arm. "We must leave. They just announced the final boarding for our flight."

Emma would have gladly missed her flight to help the rest of the people, but she felt an obligation to Fred. She knew he wouldn't leave her, and she didn't want to make him miss the flight. As he pulled her to the plane, she turned to face the remaining people still in line. "To each one of you, may the Sovereign heal you and bless you."

As Emma walked away, she took with her the full confidence that the Sovereign would do as she asked.

24

MORNING STUPOR

Emma rolled over in bed and moaned. "Just ten more minutes, Mom. Promise."

Something damp touched her cheek. She patted it. *Was I drooling again in my sleep?* A warm surge of air caressed her face. Then her cheek got wetter. She opened her eyes to see Montgomery up close, with his tongue extended for another lick. "Did you just talk to me?"

Emma, get up. The Sovereign's words formed inside Emma's mind. *You must go to your office. Now!*

Reality came into focus. Emma's mother wasn't there, trying to wake her for school. Montgomery hadn't spoken. The Sovereign had. *Do I have time to put on something more appropriate?*

Yes. Please change.

Emma slid out of bed, shimmied into her jeans, and pulled on a hoodie. She shuffled to the door, careful to not trip over anything Chloe might have strewn on the floor. She lumbered toward her office in the palace. It was barely light outside. An excited Montgomery danced along with her. Emma had forgotten his leash. Not wanting to take the time to go back, Emma snapped her fingers. "Heel Montgomery!"

He zoomed to her right, fell into step, and looked up as if to say, "How's this?"

"Good boy!"

The pair soon made it to the palace. Emma entered through the servants' door in the back and felt her way up the stairs. Down the dark hall before her, a light shone from her office. Had she been more alert, this might have worried her. But in her early morning stupor, she knew the Sovereign would protect her from whatever awaited her.

Emma paused at the doorway. Scarlett Steele was slouched over Emma's desk with her head cradled in her arms. Emma eased into the room and lay a hand on the reporter's shoulder. "Scarlett, are you all right?"

Scarlett stirred. She cocked her head to the side and opened one sleepy eye to peer up at Emma.

"Where am I?" Then she bolted upright. "What time is it?"

"It's too early for me to be up, but the Sovereign wanted me to check on you. Is everything okay?"

"I go live at eight. Where are my notes?" Scarlett shuffled through papers on the desk. Her face lit up when she retrieved the one she wanted. Then her countenance fell. "I need to run home to shower and change. I should also grab something to eat." She stood in haste and almost toppled.

Emma extended a hand to steady her friend. "You can take a shower in my room and eat in the cafeteria. But I don't think any of my clothes will fit you, so you'll need to make do with what you have. What do you think?"

Scarlett nodded. "I have a blazer in my car. I can make it work."

When they reached Emma's room, she had a warning for her friend. "Chloe's not the neatest of roommates, so watch your step."

When Emma opened the door, Scarlett shook her head. "You weren't joking."

Chloe was nowhere in sight, and the shower was running.

"Maybe this isn't such a good idea," Scarlett said. "I doubt we'll all have time to shower."

"No problem." Emma had a ready answer. "This was Barney's space. But one room wasn't big enough for him, so he connected it to the two adjoining ones. We don't use them, but there are two more showers through that door. You take the first, and I'll use the second."

MEDIA PLANS

Emma apologized to the priests for not being able to sit with them for breakfast. Then she joined Scarlett at a small table in the cafeteria's corner.

Scarlett checked the time. "In fifteen minutes, I'll go live to report on what we discovered about the Prime Minister's involvement in the death of the former High Priest and the attempt on your life." She paused. "If only you could be there so I can give you credit. But I know school is your priority."

"I don't want any credit," Emma said. "You did all the work. It's your investigation. You deserve the recognition."

Scarlett shook her head. "Let's recap. You

recommended I investigate the Prime Minister. You also recommended I investigate the protesters. Did you have any idea they were connected?"

The corner of Emma's mouth twitched up. "I suspected so but wasn't sure."

"You also told me to look for a private email account and provided the password once Lane found it. When I discovered a second account the Prime Minister used to connect with Mr. Acerman, you gave Lane that password too. Plus, you pointed out all the protesters who had broken the law or were wanted for questioning. Without you, I'd have had nothing in either investigation."

Emma shook her head. "Don't forget that you tied Acerman to funding the protest."

"Yes, but that wasn't until after you told me to 'follow the money.'"

Emma held up her hand to pray for Scarlett, which also stopped the reporter from dismissing her work. "Lord, bless Scarlett as she reports on her investigation. May she do her job with excellence. Let her know the important role she played in uncovering the Prime Minister's illegal activity. And may you receive all the glory. So be it."

Scarlett opened her eyes. "Thank you for your prayer—and the encouragement."

"That's what friends do."

Scarlett continued recapping her day's schedule. "At ten, I'll interview Frederick to talk about the Priest Academy, as well as your meeting yesterday with the Prison Oversight Authority."

Emma interrupted Scarlett. "Also be ready to react when the Prime Minister is released from the hospital. I don't know when, but I have a feeling it will happen just before lunch."

"Will do," Scarlett answered. "And this afternoon, I'll release my report about the collusion between the Prime Minister and Acerman."

Emma smiled at Scarlett's busy schedule. "May the Sovereign give you strength and fill you with energy."

26

FEDERAL AGENTS

Emma left Scarlett and her full day to dash off to school. She dropped off Montgomery at Ashley's salon.

Emma arrived at school early and began working right away, even before most of her friends had arrived. Having done most of today's schoolwork last night on the plane, Emma finished her remaining classes in about an hour. *Should I work on tomorrow's assignments, leave early, or pray?*

The Sovereign didn't give her any direction, so she lowered her head to pray.

Emma didn't know how much time had passed when two visitors interrupted her silent prayer with the Sovereign—and the rest of her classmates from their studies.

"Are you two gentlemen lost?" Jennifer moved from her desk at the front of the room toward the two men dressed in neatly tailored black suits. They looked official. They looked imposing.

"We have some questions for the High Priestess regarding her involvement with the allegations against the Prime Minister."

Jennifer moved closer to them. "I'm sure she'll be available to talk with you after lunch. As for now, you're interrupting the students and their classwork. Please leave."

"This isn't a request," the taller man said.

"It's okay," Emma told her teacher. "I'll answer their questions." She stood and walked toward them. Joshua rose and followed.

The shorter man held up his hand to stop Joshua. "Just the High Priestess."

Joshua shook his head. "I'm not leaving her alone."

"Stand down, sir," the man said. "If you persist, we will arrest you for impeding our investigation."

Joshua didn't back down. He held out his wrists in front of him. "Go ahead."

Emma touched her boyfriend's arm. "No worries, Joshua. I'll be all right." She turned her attention back to the two official-looking men. "We can meet in my office. This way, please." She brushed by them and headed out. Joshua didn't follow, but he pulled out his phone.

"Your office is currently in use by our associates in their questioning of Miss Steele," the taller man said.

"There's a small meeting room next to my office," Emma said. "We can use that. Or we can just talk right here, right now."

"That's not aligned with our protocol," the man responded. "The meeting room will be fine."

As Emma led them in that direction, Fred huffed up. "Hernandez received Joshua's text, but he didn't want to leave Scarlett alone. He sent me. Your attorney is also on her way."

The agent shook his head. "Please don't interfere with our investigation. My patience is wearing thin."

"We've been nothing but cooperative ever since you arrived," Fred said. "My job is to assist the High Priestess and protect her as needed."

The agent didn't respond and continued toward the palace.

When the four of them neared their destination, Emma glanced into her office, where Scarlett was being interviewed by two other agents. Hernandez stood by the door with his arms crossed. Though most people wouldn't be able to tell it, Emma sensed the relentless questions frazzled Scarlett, already wearied from her lack of sleep. *Bless her and give her strength*, Emma prayed silently.

One agent nudged Emma forward.

Once sitting in the meeting room, the shorter agent spoke. "Scarlett Steele reported that you provided the information about the secret email accounts and revealed the passwords. How did you obtain this information?"

Emma smiled as she leaned back in her chair. "The Sovereign told me."

"Though I respect you and revere the Sovereign," the agent said, "you can't hide behind divine revelation or even prove that it exists."

"Perhaps I can."

"I doubt it."

"Would you like a little demonstration?" Emma studied the man's face.

"Go ahead and try."

"First, your name is Carter O'Malley. Though you haven't shared this with anyone, your wife is pregnant. You'll have the son you've always wanted." Emma paused as she waited for more revelation from the Sovereign. "And you'll have the daughter your wife longs for too. You're having twins!"

The man's eyes popped open. "We won't even learn gender for another month. How could you possibly know this?"

"The Sovereign told me."

Then Emma peered at the other man. "Your name is Deimer, Darren Deimer. Though you've always wanted to be a federal agent, it's wearing on you. You wonder if you should find a job that's less demanding to give you more time with family. Possibly even moving to a more laid-back part of the country. You also—"

"That's enough!" The agent rose in his chair but settled back down. He cast a worried glance at his partner. "Please forget what you just heard." Turning back to Emma, he said, "You made your point."

The two agents looked at each other. "I think our work here is done," Deimer said to O'Malley.

"Let's confer with the rest of the team."

"You may use our conference room." Emma pointed to the space on the other side of her office.

The men headed in that direction, signaling for the two agents talking to Scarlett to join them. Not even bothering to sit, the four of them had a brief conversation and then left.

Scarlett checked the time and groaned. "I've only got seven minutes before my live interview with Frederick."

"I'm ready," Fred said, "and will help your cameraman get set up in the conference room."

27

RELEASED

As Emma had foreseen, the hospital released the Prime Minister just before noon. With much fanfare, Xtend News Network covered it live and tacked on a segment of Scarlett interviewing Emma. The piece ended with a replay of the video Emma had recorded the night before when she proclaimed healing on the Prime Minister.

When some people on social media claimed the recording of Emma was a deep fake, Scarlett posted Fred's video of the same incident to confirm it was real. That quieted the naysayers.

"You need to get some rest," Emma advised Scarlett. "Why don't you go to my room and take a quick nap?"

"I got a couple hours of sleep last night," Scarlett said. "I'll be okay."

"I insist."

Scarlett checked the time. "My next broadcast is at two. I'm going to expose the collusion between the Prime Minister and G. S. Acerman."

Emma tugged at Scarlett's arm. "I'll wake you in plenty of time."

As Scarlett slept, Emma prayed. She woke her friend at quarter to two.

Emma hastily picked up Chloe's clothes strewn around the room, while the cameraman set up to shoot the segment in the sitting area in Emma's room. It would make for a professional setting and give viewers a different backdrop from the day's two earlier broadcasts.

When the cameraman signaled her to begin, Scarlett shared her findings of collusion between the powerful billionaire and the Prime Minister. She even quoted a couple of passages from their secret communication. "This all happened because of the High Priestess," Scarlett said. "Emma even revealed the password so I could access the information."

Emma hadn't expected Scarlett to mention her role in the investigation, but supernatural peace filled her as she explained. "It wasn't a password but a pass phrase. The Sovereign gave me direction on where to look. I recalled an odd phrase the Prime Minister had used when we talked. It turns out those were the exact words that gave Scarlett access."

"There you have it," Scarlett concluded. "Without the High Priestess's help, we'd have never uncovered this terrible corruption at the highest level in our government. This is Scarlett Steele reporting for Xtend News Network." Then her face brightened. "As Emma would say, may you have a blessed day!"

Two hours later, federal agents arrested the Prime Minister.

At 4:30, the sponsors withdrew their bill against the Temple school. Just before five, Senator Warren announced he would likewise cancel his bill that would prohibit Emma from being High Priestess.

28

LAST CHANCE

Emma awoke in the middle of the night. It was 3:00. She thought about the Prime Minister. Emma wanted to urge her to repent and turn to the Sovereign.

Just as Emma had connected with Gabe and Joshua's spirit in the past, Emma reached out to connect with the Prime Minister's. After much searching, Emma located her, but she barred Emma from interaction.

Is it possible for me to approach the Prime Minister in the spiritual realm? Emma asked the Sovereign. *Barney and the Prime Minister both did it to me without my permission. How do I do that?*

Just as your spirit can leave your body to visit me in

heaven, your spirit can leave your body to interact with someone in the spiritual realm.

Emma slowed her breathing and focused on her spirit. In seconds, her essence eased away from her shell. Instead of moving upward toward heaven, Emma sped eastward toward the capital. But she wouldn't attack the Prime Minister. She just wanted to talk.

Emma slowed her movement as she approached the jet-black blob of the Prime Minister's spirit.

Shocked at Emma's presence, the Prime Minister's spirit puffed up to protect herself.

"I only want to talk," Emma said.

"I don't," the Prime Minister responded.

"Just listen."

The Prime Minister didn't respond.

"Though your political career is over," Emma said, "I'm concerned about your place in eternity. Turn to the Sovereign and receive divine forgiveness."

"I will never turn," came the Prime Minister's quick response. "Dark is more powerful than light."

"How's that been working out for you?"

The dark black of the Prime Minister's spirit fled from Emma's presence.

If you enjoyed *Pursuing the Politicians*, please leave a review online. Your review will help others learn about this book and encourage them to read it too.

Thank you.

RESTORING THE REPENTANT

BOOK 9 IN THE NEXT HIGH PRIEST SERIES

Chapter 1: A Dubious Meeting

Emma waited for Jennifer by her teacher's car. They had an unusual relationship, but it worked. At first Jennifer was Emma's food server, but Emma soon changed that. Now Jennifer was Emma's instructor at their microschool in the mornings. The rest of the time they interacted as friends, even though Jennifer was ten years older. Overshadowing all this was the reality that Emma was also Jennifer's boss—actually her boss's boss. Despite all this, they got along just fine.

Emma groaned. She didn't want to do this. But

she had to. She shifted from her right foot to her left and back again.

She'd only waited a few minutes when David's sports car roared up. From the passenger seat, Jennifer leaned over and gave her boyfriend a quick kiss. She jumped out and headed to her car as David rumbled away.

"I still can't believe they arrested the Prime Minister." Jennifer shook her head. "You and Scarlett were brilliant in uncovering her conspiring to kill you . . . along with all her other crimes."

"Scarlett did the investigative reporting," Emma said. "I merely told her what the Sovereign had told me."

"Your humble spirit is one of the many things that draw people to you," Jennifer said. "First Barney Clark was arrested for trying to kill you. Then the seven rebellious priests were arrested for receiving stolen Temple funds. And now the Prime Minister." Jennifer chuckled. "People should realize now that if they get in your way, you'll take them out."

"I turn them over to the Sovereign for judgment," Emma said. "It's not my job to punish."

Jennifer unlocked her car and climbed in. Emma walked around to the other side and slid in.

Jennifer started the engine and drove toward their destination.

"Are you sure you want to do this?" the teacher asked the student.

Emma considered her answer before speaking. In truth, she didn't. "Yes." She confirmed her answer with a decided downward tip of her head.

"So I can't talk you out of it?"

"Nope."

"Have you discussed this with anyone?" Jennifer asked.

"Hernandez said it was a bad idea," Emma replied.

"Given that he's your head of security, that makes sense. What about Frederick?"

"He said I didn't have to do it and wouldn't blame me if I didn't."

"That makes sense too. As your executive admin, he'd need to deal with any fallout. What about Joshua?"

"Didn't ask," Emma said. "I knew he'd be against it but would insist on tagging along anyway."

"You should be happy to have a boyfriend who wants to protect you and keep you safe."

"I am. I really am. But sometimes he's too protective."

"Not to be critical," Jennifer said, "but a failure to communicate has caused problems with you two in the past. Like when he went undercover to find out where the prisoners were being held when you didn't want him to."

Emma groaned. "I ordered him not to do it. I can't believe I played the High Priestess card on him. Then I ignored him for a couple of days."

Jennifer was right. Every problem in Emma and Joshua's short relationship was because of a lack of communication—mostly on Emma's part. She'd need to do better. But now that she'd already committed to this dubious meeting, it was too late to correct her mistake this time.

Jennifer continued her gentle counsel. "Don't forget that David and I spent three years away from each other, all because we didn't communicate. If you hadn't intervened and gotten us back together, we'd still be apart today."

"I guess it's easier to see other people's problems than my own," Emma said. "Let me know the next time you see me messing up."

"You can count on it," Jennifer said. "One more

question. What did Gabe say about all this? He's your spiritual mentor, after all."

"At first, he wasn't in favor of it either," Emma said. "But once he knew the Sovereign told me to do it, he was completely behind me."

"Wait just a minute! The Sovereign told you to do this? You should've led with that."

"Gabe's praying for me right now. That I'll have the strength to do what the Sovereign told me to do."

"I'll also pray for you during your meeting."

Emma shifted in her seat, not that she was uncomfortable—at least not in a physical sense. She changed the subject. "How have things been going with you and David?"

"We couldn't be better." Jennifer let out a happy sigh. "I did as you suggested and proclaimed that the Sovereign's Divine Spirit fill him. And it happened! I still don't understand it, but we're now at the same place spiritually."

"So you're ready to get married?"

"Most definitely." Jennifer's head bobbed with excitement. "We really like how you officiated Ashley and Topher's wedding on Saturday. It was simple yet meaningful. We agree with your focus on marriage as a lifelong commitment made in front of family, friends, and the Sovereign."

"The Holy Text says the Sovereign hates divorce. The key to a good marriage is to be faithful and commit to push through the hard times together." Emma grinned, a response that started in her mind and bloomed on her face. "And, of course, good communication."

"Before we pick a date, we'd like a married couple to do some pre-wedding mentoring with us," Jennifer said. "Do you have any suggestions?"

"Great idea." Emma searched her mind, thinking aloud. "None of the priests are married . . . yet. That's not an option. Olivia has the training, but she's single too. I suspect some of our married staff would be open to mentoring you, but I'm not sure who to ask. Although . . ."

"Although who?" Jennifer asked.

"Maybe my parents," Emma said. "They have a great relationship. I've learned a lot from watching them. I'll email them."

"Wouldn't a text be quicker?"

"Mom prefers email."

By the time Emma had sent the message, Jennifer had arrived at their destination. She pulled into the prison parking lot and stopped in front of the visitors' entrance.

Buoyed by her confidence in the Sovereign, Emma strode through the doors, cleared security, and marched to the counter. "I'm here to see Barney Clark."

Continue Emma's adventure in *Restoring the Repentant*, book 9 of The Next High Priest Series.

ABOUT PETER DEHAAN

Peter DeHaan is an adult who dreams of being a teenager. When he's not contemplating grown-up thoughts, his mind retreats to the domain of invented worlds with his loyal and most real, yet still imaginary, friends. What grand adventures they have: righting wrongs, solving problems, and making their world a better place to live.

His first published adventures come to life in "The Next High Priest Series"—a faith-friendly speculative fiction adventure in a world just like ours . . . only different.

Next up is *The Curious Gift*, a YA contemporary novella with a hint of the supernatural.

Then comes "The Ice Creamed Series," a present-day quest for friendship and love, all the while trying to survive high school unscathed and ping-ponging between responsible impulses and irresponsible slipups.

Want more? Get a free short-story prequel about Emma along with news of upcoming books when you sign up to receive updates at PeterDeHaan.com/fiction.

FICTION BOOKS BY PETER DEHAAN

The Next High Priest Series

Seeking the Sovereign

Confronting the Chaos

Dueling the Devil

Reforming the Religion

Freeing the Prisoners

Fighting the Fanatics

Perfecting the Priesthood

Pursuing the Politicians

Restoring the Repentant

Learn more at PeterDeHaan.com/fiction.